Two Symphonies

ANDRÉ GIDE

Two Symphonies

*Translated from the French
by Dorothy Bussy*

VINTAGE BOOKS
A DIVISION OF RANDOM HOUSE
NEW YORK

FIRST VINTAGE BOOKS EDITION, August 1977
Copyright 1931 by Alfred A. Knopf, Inc.
Copyright renewed 1959 by Alfred A. Knopf, Inc.

Library of Congress Cataloging in Publication Data

Gide, André Paul Guillaume, 1869-1951.
　Two symphonies

　Originally published in 1931 by Knopf, New York.
　CONTENTS: Isabelle.—The pastoral symphony.
　I. Gide, André Paul Guillaume, 1869-1951.
La symphonie pastorale. 1977. II. Title.
PZ3.G3613Tw7 [PQ2613.I2]　843'.9'12　77-4750
ISBN 0-394-72454-2

ISABELLE

TO
ANDRÉ RUYTERS

GÉRARD LACASE, with whom Francis Jammes and I were staying in the August of 189—, took us one day to see the château of La Quartfourche, which even then was hardly more than a ruin. It stood in a great deserted park where summer was lavishing its glories with unrestrained prodigality. Nothing remained to forbid intrusion—neither the half-filled boundary ditch, nor the broken-down hedges, nor the iron park gates, which hung on loosened hinges and yielded crazily to our first push. No trace of paths was left; a few cows had been let loose to graze on the unkempt luxuriant grass of the overgrown lawns, and others were seeking shelter from the sun in the cool hollows now gutted of their trees; in the midst of this wild profusion it was only here and there that some flower or rare foliage could be distinguished—patient remnants of former cultivation, but now almost smothered out of existence by the invasion of more vulgar species. We followed Gérard without speaking, oppressed by the beauty of the place, the season, and the hour, and feeling, too, all the neglect and heartache that perhaps lay hidden under this excessive opulence. The perron

3

—the lower steps of which were swamped in grass
and the upper cracked and disjointed—was soon
reached; but when we tried to get into the drawing-
room, the barred shutters of the French windows
stopped us. We entered the house at last like thieves,
by crawling through one of the cellar lights; a flight
of steps led up to the kitchens; not one of the inside doors was shut . . . and as we passed from
room to room—walking warily, for the sagging
floors looked as if they might give way beneath us
at any moment—we stifled the sound of our steps,
not that we thought there was anyone to hear them,
but because the noise of our presence re-echoing
through the profound silence of the empty house
sounded unseemly and almost alarming. Several
panes were missing in the ground-floor windows, and
a bignonia had thrust its huge white flabby stalks
through the slats of the shutters into the dusky half-
light of the dining-room.

Gérard had left us; he had known the former
owners of the house and we thought he might prefer
to revisit the place alone, so we continued our in-
spection without him. No doubt he had gone up to
the first floor and passed before us through the bare
and desolate rooms; in one of them a small branch
of box was still hanging on the wall from a kind of
hook to which it was tied by a bit of faded ribbon; it

seemed to be swinging slightly at the end of its loop and I thought to myself that Gérard must just have pulled a twig from it as he passed by.

We came across him again in a passage on the second floor. There was no glass in the window beside which he was standing, and a dangling rope had been pulled through it from the outside; it was a bell-rope and I was on the point of giving it a gentle pull when I felt Gérard seize my arm; his action, instead of stopping mine, only accentuated it: a hoarse clang suddenly rang out; it sounded so near us and so harsh that it made us start; then, when silence seemed to have quite closed in again, one more note and after it another dropped slowly down, pure and distant. I looked at Gérard and saw his lips were trembling.

"Let's come away," he said; "I can't breathe here."

As soon as we were outside, he excused himself for not accompanying us; there was someone in the neighborhood he wanted to inquire after. We understood from his tone of voice that it would be indiscreet to follow him, so Jammes and I returned alone to La R., where Gérard joined us in the course of the evening.

"My dear fellow," said Jammes after a time, "let me warn you that I am determined not to tell you the smallest tale until you come out with the one you obviously have on your mind."

Now, Jammes's tales were the delight of our evenings.

"I would willingly tell you the story the scene of which was laid in the house you saw this afternoon," began Gérard, "but I was only able to discover or reconstruct it partially; besides, I am afraid that if I attempt to tell it in any sort of order, I shall strip it of all the attraction of baffling mystery with which my curiosity invested each event as it occurred."

"Put as little order into your story as you please," said Jammes.

"Why should one try to rearrange facts in their chronological sequence?" added I. "Why not put them before us just as you discovered them?"

"Then you must allow me to talk a great deal about myself," said Gérard.

"Which of us ever does anything else?" was Jammes's rejoinder.

This is the story Gérard told us.

i

I CAN hardly understand nowadays the impatience with which I then flung myself upon life. At twenty-five years of age I knew almost nothing of it except from books; and that no doubt is why I thought myself a novelist; for I had not as yet realized how cunningly and maliciously events conceal from us just that part of themselves most likely to interest us, and how slight a handle they offer the man who is incapable of wresting their secret from them by force.

I was at that time preparing a thesis on the chronology of Bossuet's sermons, with a view to my doctor's degree; not that I was particularly attracted by pulpit oratory; I had chosen the subject out of deference to my old master Albert Desnos, who had just completed the publication of his great *Life of Bossuet*. As soon as M. Desnos heard of my plans, he offered to assist me in gaining access to the material. One of his oldest friends, Benjamin Floche, of the Académie des Inscriptions et Belles-Lettres, possessed various documents that would no doubt be of use to me, and in particular a Bible covered with annotations in Bossuet's own handwriting. M. Floche, who had retired about fifteen years earlier to La Quartfourche, more commonly known as Le Carrefour, or the Crossways, an old family estate in the neighborhood of Pont-l'Évêque, from which he never stirred and where he would be delighted to receive me and put at my service his papers, his library, and his learning—which M. Desnos said was inexhaustible.

Letters were exchanged between M. Desnos and M. Floche. The documents, it appeared, were more numerous than my master had at first led me to expect; there was soon no question of a mere afternoon's visit; M. Floche was kind enough, on the recommendation of M. Desnos, to invite me to stay for a while at the château of La Quartfourche. Although M. and Mme Floche had no children, they did not live alone; a few careless words let fall by M. Desnos fired my imagination and filled me with the hope of meeting company there far more attractive than any dusty documents of the seventeenth century; my thesis soon became a mere pretext; it was no longer as a scholar that I proposed to visit the château, but as a Nezhdanov,[1] as a Valmont;[2]

---

[1] *Nezhdanov*, hero of *Virgin Soil* by Turgenyev.

[2] *Valmont*, hero of *Les Liaisons dangereuses* by Laclos.

I peopled it with adventures. La Quartfourche! The Crossways! I repeated the mysterious name again and again. "This," thought I, "is the scene of Hercules' hesitation. . . . I know indeed what awaits him on the path of virtue; but what of the other road? . . . the other road. . . ."

Toward the middle of September I put together the best of my modest wardrobe, replenished my selection of ties, and started.

When I reached the station of Breuil-Blangy, between Pont-l'Évêque and Lisieux, it was already night. I was the only person to get out of the train. A sort of peasant dressed in livery came up to me, took my bag, and escorted me to the carriage that was waiting on the other side of the station. The appearance of the horse and carriage cut short any flights of imagination. A more lamentable turnout cannot be conceived. The peasant coachman went to fetch my trunk, which I had registered, and the springs of the old barouche sank under its weight. Inside there was a suffocating smell of poultry. . . . I tried to let down the window, and the strap came off in my hand. There had been rain during the day and the roads were heavy; at the bottom of the first hill a part of the harness gave way. The coachman pulled a bit of string from under the seat and set to work doctoring the trace. I had got out of the carriage and offered to hold the carriage lamp he had just lighted; I could see that the poor man's livery, like the harness, had more than once been in need of patching.

"The leather is a bit old," I hazarded.

He looked at me as if I had insulted him and answered almost brutally:

"It was lucky for you, mister, we were able to come for you."

"Is the château far?" I asked in my gentlest voice. He made no direct answer to my question, but: "You may be sure it's not a journey we do every day!" he growled. Then, after a moment: "It's a matter of six months maybe that the carriage hasn't been out. . . ."

"Oh! Your masters don't go driving often?" I went on, in a desperate effort to keep the conversation going.

"No, indeed! As if there weren't other things to do!"

The damage was repaired by now and he motioned me to get into the carriage, which set off again.

The horse labored up the hills, stumbled down them, and shambled horribly along the flat; at times he suddenly stopped dead.

"If we go on in this way," I thought, "we shan't get to the Crossways till long after my hosts have finished dinner; and even"—here the horse stopped again—"after they have gone to bed." I was very hungry and my temper was beginning to suffer. I tried to look at the landscape; without my having noticed it, the carriage had left the highroad and turned into a rough, narrow lane; the carriage lamps cast their light right and left on thick, high, uninterrupted hedges; they seemed to enclose us, to bar the road, to open out only just in time to let us through, and then the moment after to close up again behind us.

At the foot of a rather steeper hill the carriage stopped once more. The coachman came to the door, opened it, and said without further apology:

"Please get down, mister. The hill is a bit steep for the horse." He took the poor jade by the bridle and set off walking beside it. Halfway up the hill he turned round toward me as I was bringing up the rear.

"We shall soon be there now," he said in a milder tone. "Look! There's the park." And I saw in front of us a dark mass of trees blotting out part of the unclouded sky. It was an avenue of great beeches; we turned into it and struck the wider road we had left. The coachman invited me to get back into the carriage, and we soon reached the gate and turned into the garden.

It was too dark for me to make out the front of the château; the carriage set me down before a perron of three or four steps, which I went up, slightly dazed by a light that a woman was holding in her hand and casting down on me. She was of no particular age, plain, thickset, and shabbily dressed. She gave me rather a stiff nod. I bowed in some uncertainty. . . .

"Madame Floche, no doubt? . . ."

"No, only Mademoiselle Verdure. Monsieur and Madame Floche have gone to bed. They beg you to excuse them for not being here to receive you; but we dine early."

"But you, mademoiselle? I'm afraid I have kept you up late."

"Oh, I'm accustomed to it," she said without turning round. She had preceded me into the hall. "Perhaps you would like to take something?"

"I must admit I haven't dined."

She showed me into a vast dining-room, where a respectable supper was laid out.

"At this time of night the kitchen fire is out; and in the country one must put up with what one can get."

"But it all looks excellent," I said, sitting down to a plate of cold meat. She herself settled sideways on a chair near the door; and during the whole time I was eating she stayed there, her eyes lowered, her hands crossed on her knees, in the deliberately assumed attitude of an underling. Several times when there was a pause in our uphill conversation, I apologized for detaining her; but she gave me to understand that she was waiting to clear away after I had finished.

"And how would you find your room all by yourself?"

I was making as much haste as I could and taking double-sized mouthfuls when the door into the hall opened and a gray-haired priest with a rude-featured but pleasant face came in. He came toward me with outstretched hand.

"I was not going to put off the pleasure of welcoming our guest till tomorrow. I did not come down sooner because I knew you were talking to Mademoiselle Olympe Verdure," he said, turning toward her with what looked like a teasing smile, while she sat with pursed-up lips and a wooden

expression on her countenance. "But now that you
have finished eating," he went on as I rose, "we
will leave Mademoiselle Olympe to put things
tidy; she will think it more proper, I presume, to
allow a man to conduct Monsieur Lacase to his
bedroom and will resign that function to me."

He bowed ceremoniously to Mlle Verdure, who
returned him a perfunctory curtsy.

"Oh! I resign; I resign. . . . I always resign to
you, Monsieur l'Abbé, as you know. . . ." Then
she suddenly turned back:

"You were going to make me forget to ask Monsieur Lacase what he takes for breakfast."

"Whatever you like, mademoiselle. . . . What
is the usual thing here?"

"Oh, anything. Tea for the ladies, coffee for Monsieur Floche, a plate of soup for Monsieur l'Abbé,
and cereal for Monsieur Casimir."

"And you, mademoiselle, do you take nothing?"

"Oh, I? Just *café au lait*."

"If you will allow me, I will join you in taking
café au lait."

"Oho! Be careful, mademoiselle," said the Abbé,
taking me by the arm. "It looks to me very much
as if Monsieur Lacase were making love to you!"

She shrugged her shoulders, then bowed to me
quickly, while the Abbé carried me off.

My room was on the second floor, almost at the end of a passage.

"Here," said the Abbé, opening the door of a spacious room in which a large wood fire was burning. "God bless my soul! They've given you a fire. I dare say you would as soon have done without it. . . . It's true the nights in this part of the world are damp, and the season this year is unusually rainy."

He went up to the hearth, stretching out his huge hands toward the blaze, while at the same time he turned aside his face, in the attitude of a man of virtue warding off temptation. He seemed more inclined to talk than to let me sleep.

"So," he began, catching sight of my trunk and handbag, "Gratien has brought up your luggage."

"Is Gratien the coachman who drove me here?" I asked.

"And the gardener too; for his duties as coachman cannot be said to take up much of his time."

"Yes, he told me the barouche did not go out very often."

"It's a historical event every time it goes out. Besides, Monsieur de Saint-Auréol gave up his stables long ago; on grand occasions like tonight they borrow the farmer's horse."

"Monsieur de Saint-Auréol?" I repeated in surprise.

"Yes," he said; "I know that it is Monsieur Floche you have come to see, but La Quartfourche belongs to his brother-in-law. Tomorrow you will have the honor of being presented to Monsieur and Madame de Saint-Auréol."

"And who is the Monsieur Casimir who takes cereal for breakfast—the only thing I know about him?"

"Their grandson and my pupil. By God's permission, I have had charge of his education for the last three years." He said this with his eyes closed and an air of devout humility as if he were talking of a prince of the blood.

"Aren't his parents here?" I asked.

"Traveling." He screwed up his lips and went on at once: "I know, monsieur, what noble, pious work brings you here. . . ."

"Oh, don't exaggerate its piety," I interrupted, laughing. "I am only interested in it from a historical point of view."

"No matter," said he, wafting aside any unpleasantness with a wave of his hand; "history has its rights too. You will find Monsieur Floche the kindest and the surest of guides."

"So my master, Monsieur Desnos, assured me."

"Ah! You are a pupil of Albert Desnos?" He screwed up his lips again.

"Did you ever attend his lectures?" I had the imprudence to inquire.

"No," he answered roughly. "I know enough about him to be on my guard. . . . An intellectual adventurer. At your age one is easily led astray by anything out of the ordinary. . . ." And as I did not answer, "His theories," he went on, "began by having some influence over the young; but it is already on the wane, I hear."

I was much more inclined to sleep than to argue. Seeing he could not extract an answer out of me, he went on:

"Monsieur Floche's guidance will be less dangerous."

Then, in face of a yawn I did not attempt to disguise, "It's getting late," he said. "Tomorrow, if you allow it, we shall find time to continue our conversation. After your journey you must be tired."

"I confess, Monsieur l'Abbé, I am dropping with sleep."

As soon as he had left me, I took the logs off the fire, opened the window wide, and flung back the shutters. A great rush of dark, damp air blew down the flame of my candle and I put it out so as better to contemplate the night. My room gave on to the

park, but it was not on the front side of the house
like those in the long passage, from which the view
was no doubt more extensive; mine was interrupted
immediately by a mass of trees; there was barely
a little space of sky left above them, in which the
moon's crescent appeared for a moment, only to be
hidden again the next by clouds. There had been
more rain; the branches were still showering
tears. . . .

"All this doesn't seem to promise a very gay
time," thought I as I closed the window and shutters. My moment's contemplation had chilled me
through and through—soul even more than body.
I piled on the logs again, made up the fire, and was
delighted to find a hot-water bottle in my bed,
placed there, no doubt, by the kind attention of
Mlle Verdure.

A moment later it occurred to me I had forgotten to put my shoes outside the door. I got up and
stepped for a second into the passage; Mlle Verdure was going by at the other end of the house.
Her room was above mine, as I gathered from the
heavy footstep that shortly after began to shake
my ceiling. Then a profound silence followed and,
as I sank to sleep, the house weighed anchor and
started on its passage through the night.

ii

I WAS WAKENED quite early by sounds from the kitchen, one door of which was immediately under my window. I pushed open the shutters and saw with delight an almost perfectly clear sky; the garden was still wet and glittering from a recent shower, and a bluish haze colored the air. I was just going to shut my window again when a boy came running out of the vegetable garden toward the kitchen. It was difficult to guess his age, for his face looked three or four years older than the rest of his body, which was badly deformed; his twisted legs gave him the most peculiar lurching gait, and he progressed obliquely, or rather by a series of springs, almost as if he had a difficulty in getting one foot safely past the other. Obviously this must be Casimir, the Abbé's pupil. An enormous Newfoundland dog kept him company, gamboling at his side and jumping up at him with boisterous affection. The child kept him off as best he could, but just as they reached the kitchen, the dog, with a sudden bound, knocked him completely over and sent him rolling in the mud. A stout kitchen wench darted out, exclaiming as she picked the child up:

"Well I never! A nice mess you're in now! Lord, how does the boy manage it! Ain't you been told scores o' times to leave Terno in the stable? Come along in with you and get wiped. . . ."

She dragged him into the kitchen. Just then there was a knock at my door; a maid had brought me my hot water. A quarter of an hour later the breakfast bell rang.

As I entered the dining-room, "Madame Floche," said the Abbé, coming forward to meet me, "here, I think, is our kind visitor."

Mme Floche had risen from her chair, but seemed no taller standing than sitting. I made her a low bow, which she returned with an abrupt little bob. Some time or other some terrible event must have descended upon her and driven her head down between her shoulders, where it had remained ever since—and a little crooked too. M. Floche had come to her side to shake hands with me. The little old couple were of exactly the same height, dressed after the same fashion; they looked the same age,

seemed to be of one flesh. . . . For a few moments
we stood exchanging vague compliments, all three
talking at once. Then a majestic silence fell and
Mlle Verdure came in carrying the teapot.

"Mademoiselle Olympe," said Mme Floche at
last (she was incapable of moving her head and
therefore turned to address one from the waist upwards), "our friend, Mademoiselle Olympe, was
very anxious to know if you had slept well, and
whether your bed was quite to your liking."

I protested that it would have been impossible
to sleep better and that the hot-water bottle I had
found in my bed had been the greatest of comforts.

Then Mlle Verdure, having wished me good-
morning, went out again.

"And the noise from the kitchen didn't disturb
you too much this morning?"

I renewed my protestations.

"Do not hesitate to complain, I beg of you, for
it would be perfectly easy to get another room
ready. . . ."

M. Floche, without saying anything himself,
nodded his head sideways and confirmed every
word of his wife's with a smile.

"I can see it must be a very large house," said I,
"but I assure you I could not be more comfortably
lodged."

"Monsieur and Madame Floche," said the Abbé, "take pleasure in spoiling their guests."

Mlle Olympe now brought in a plate of toast, pushing before her the little cripple whose tumble I had so lately witnessed. The Abbé seized him by the arm.

"Now then, Casimir, come along! You're not a baby now; come and say how-d'ye-do to Monsieur Lacase like a man. Put out your hand. Look up!" Then turning to me as if some excuse were necessary: "We're not much used to company yet."

The child's shyness made me feel uncomfortable.

"Is he your grandson?" I asked Mme Floche, quite forgetting the Abbé's information of the previous evening.

"Our great-nephew," she replied; "you will shortly be seeing my brother-in-law and my sister, who are his grandparents."

"He was afraid to come in because he had got his clothes muddy, playing with Terno," explained Mlle Verdure.

"It was a funny kind of game," said I, turning sympathetically to Casimir. "I was at the window when he knocked you over. Didn't he hurt you?"

"We must let Monsieur Lacase know," explained the Abbé in his turn, "that a good balance is not one of our strong points. . . ."

I could see that for myself, good heavens, without its being necessary for him to point it out. And
I took an immediate dislike to this great strapping,
wall-eyed Abbé.

The child had given me no answer, but his face
turned crimson. I was sorry for what I had said
and afraid he might think I had meant some allusion to his infirmity. The Abbé, having finished his
soup, had risen and was walking up and down the
room. When not speaking he had a way of tightly
closing his mouth so that it looked like the
pursed-up, toothless mouth of a very old man. He
came to a standstill behind Casimir, who was just
scraping out his bowl.

"Come along, come along, young man! Avenzoar awaits us!"

The boy got up and they went out together.

As soon as breakfast was over, M. Floche beckoned to me.

"Come with me into the garden, my young friend,
and tell me how it fares with the world of intellectual Paris."

M. Floche's eloquence rose with the lark. Without paying much attention to my answers, he asked
after his friend Gaston Boissier and various other

learned men whom I might have studied under and
with whom he still corresponded from time to time.
He questioned me on my tastes, my studies. I naturally said nothing about my literary projects and
all I showed him of myself was the Sorbonne
scholar. He then embarked on the history of La
Quartfourche, from which place he had not stirred
for nearly fifteen years—on the history, that is, of
the park and house; the history of the family who
had occupied it formerly was reserved for a later
recital, but he began to tell me how he had become the possessor of certain seventeenth-century
manuscripts that he thought might prove useful
for my thesis. . . . His steps, as he walked, or
rather trotted, beside me, were very short and hurried. I noticed he wore his trousers so low that the
fork came half way down his thigh; the stuff hung
in folds over his instep in front, but at the back,
kept up by Heaven knows what mysterious de-
vice, it barely reached the top of his shoes. By this
time, bemused by the soft warmth of the air and a
kind of vegetable torpor, I was lending him a somewhat inattentive ear. We had followed an avenue
of great chestnuts whose branches met overhead,
and come out almost at the other end of the park.
There was a bench there, shaded from the sun by

a bush of smoke tree,[1] and M. Floche invited me to sit down.

"Did Abbé Santal tell you," he began abruptly, "that my brother-in-law was a little—?" He did not finish the sentence, but touched his forehead with his forefinger.

I was too much taken aback to be able to think of anything to answer. He continued:

"Yes, the Baron de Saint-Auréol, my brother-in-law. Perhaps the Abbé has not told you so any more than he has me . . . but all the same I know he thinks it; and so do I. . . . And about me, didn't the Abbé tell you I was a little—?"

"Oh, Monsieur Floche, how can you imagine—?"

"But, my dear young man," said he, tapping me confidentially on the hand, "I should think it only natural. Why not? We have fallen into habits down here, by shutting ourselves up so far from the world, which may be a little—out of the way perhaps. Nothing in the shape of—what shall I call it?—diversion, reaches us here. Yes indeed. It was very kind of you to come and see us"—and as I attempted a movement in protest—"I repeat, very kind, and I shall write this evening to my good friend Desnos and tell him so again: but if you

---

[1] *Rhus cotinus*, a kind of sumach, sometimes called *wig tree*.

had any notion of confiding in me the things you have most at heart, the questions that trouble you, the problems that interest you—well, I feel sure I should not understand what you were saying."

What answer could I make? I scratched the gravel with the end of my stick.

"You see," he continued, "we have lost touch a little down here. No, no! There's no need to protest. The Baron is as deaf as a post, but he's so vain that all he cares for is not to appear so; he had rather pretend to hear than make people speak louder. As for me, with regard to the opinions of the day, I believe I am as deaf as he; and as far as that goes, I don't complain. I don't really much try to understand. My long intercourse with Massillon and Bossuet has led me to believe that the problems that exercised their great minds are quite as noble and important as those which engrossed me in my youth—problems that their minds, great as they were, would certainly not have been able to understand—any more than I am able to understand those that engross you today. Therefore, with your consent, my dear colleague to be, you shall talk to me by preference of your studies, as they happen to be mine too, and you will forgive me if I do not question you as to the musicians, the poets, or the orators you admire, nor as to the form of government you consider best."

He took out an ancient large cheap watch fastened to a black ribbon and looked at the time.

"Let us go in now," said he, getting up. "I feel my day is lost if I am not at work by ten o'clock."

I offered him my arm, which he took, and if at moments I happened to slacken my pace on his account, "Hasten! Hasten!" he would bid me. "Thoughts are like flowers; those gathered in the morning keep fresh the longest."

The library at La Quartfourche consists of two rooms separated only by a curtain. One, exceedingly small and raised by three steps above the other, is where M. Floche works, at a table in front of a window. There is no view—nothing but the branches of elm or alder brushing against the panes. On the table stands an old-fashioned oil lamp with a green porcelain shade; under the table, a huge foot-muff; in one corner a little stove; in the other a second table piled with lexicons; between the two a cupboard fitted as a filing cabinet. The second room is immense; its walls are lined to the ceiling with books; it has two windows; a big table stands in the center.

"This is where you are to sit," said M. Floche; and as I uttered an exclamation, "No, no! I am used to my little den," he said; "to tell you the truth, it suits me best; I feel I can concentrate better here. Do not scruple to use the big table, and, if you like, we can draw the curtain so as not to disturb each other."

"Not on my account," I protested; "if I had had to be alone all this time in order to work, I should never—"

"Very well," he replied without letting me finish, "then we will leave it undrawn. For my part, it will be a great pleasure to be able to catch a glimpse of you now and then out of the corner of my eye."

(And, as a fact, in the days that followed I never lifted my head from my work without meeting the old fellow's eye. He would smile and nod at me, or hurriedly look the other way for fear of disturbing me, and pretend to be deep in his reading.)

He set to work at once, arranging the books and manuscripts likely to interest me so that I could most easily get at them. They were kept for the most part in the filing cabinet in the little room; their number and importance greatly surpassed the account M. Desnos had given me of them; it would take me a week at least, I could see, to extract all

the treasures of information they contained. Finally
M. Floche opened a very small cupboard next the
cabinet and took out of it the famous "Bossuet
Bible," in which, opposite the verses he had used
as texts, the Eagle of Meaux had inscribed the dates
of the sermons they had inspired. I expressed astonishment that Albert Desnos had made no use of
these entries in his writings; but the book had only
recently come into M. Floche's hands.

"As a matter of fact, I did write a memoir on the
subject," he continued, "and am glad now not to
have communicated it to anyone yet, as it may
prove useful to you for your thesis and will be entirely new."

Again I expostulated:

"Whatever merit my thesis may have, I shall
owe it to your kindness. I hope at least I may be
allowed to dedicate it to you, Monsieur Floche, as
a very small mark of my gratitude."

He smiled a little sadly.

"When one is so near leaving this world, one
gives a welcome to anything that promises any
kind of survival."

I felt it would have been unsuitable for me to
improve upon this.

"And now," he went on, "you will take possession of the library and only remember my pres-

ence if there is anything you want to ask me.
Take the papers you want with you. . . . Au revoir! . . ." And as I went down the three steps and
turned my head to smile at him, he waved his hand
in return: "Au revoir!"

I carried off with me into the big room the necessary papers with which to start my work. Without leaving the table at which I sat I could still
see M. Floche in his little "den." He fidgeted about
for a few minutes, opening and shutting drawers,
pulling out papers and putting them back, with
all the appearance of being a very busy man. . . .
I could not help suspecting that he was a good deal
disturbed, not to say put out, by my presence and
that in his usually well-ordered existence the slightest shock was likely to endanger his mental equi-
librium. At last he settled down, plunged knee-deep
into the foot-muff and remained motionless. . . .

I also made a pretense of being absorbed in my
work, but I found it very difficult to control my
thoughts; I did not even attempt to. Those thoughts
of mine went circling round La Quartfourche as if
it were a fortress the entrance to which I had perforce to find. Was I subtle?—that was what I
wished to be sure of. "Now, my friend," said I to

myself, "you would-be writer of novels, we shall see what you are made of! Description? Heaven forbid! That is not what is wanted here, but to discover the reality beneath the semblance. . . . In the short space of time allowed you for your stay at La Quartfourche, if you let one gesture escape you—one twitch even—without immediately accounting for it to yourself, psychologically, historically, and completely, it will be because you don't know your job."

And I once more turned to look at M. Floche; he sat with his profile toward me and I saw a big flabby, inexpressive nose, bushy eyebrows, a clean-shaven chin, continually on the move as though chewing a quid . . . and I thought that nothing can make a face more impenetrable than the mask of kindliness.

The luncheon bell surprised me in the midst of these reflections.

iii

IT WAS AT that same lunch that M. Floche, without a word of oratorical warning, led me into the presence of the Saint-Auréol couple. The Abbé at least might have dropped me a hint the night before. I remember having experienced the same feeling of stupefaction once upon a time at the Zoological Gardens, when I first made the acquaintance of the *Phœnicopterus antiquorum,* or the spatula-beaked flamingo.[1] It is impossible to say whether the Baron or the Baronne was the more peculiar; they made a perfect pair—like the Floches, for that matter; in a museum they would have been placed in the same glass case without a moment's hesitation and labeled "extinct species." When I first saw them, I experienced the same kind of ill-defined admiration that fills one on first seeing a perfectly accomplished work of art or one of the

---

[1] Gérard is mistaken; the beak of the *Phœnicopterus antiquorum* is not spatula-shaped. (Author's note.)

wonders of nature—things that leave one stupid
with amazement and incapable of any analysis of
one's feelings. It was only gradually that I managed
to unravel my impressions. . . .

Baron Narcisse de Saint-Auréol wore knee-
breeches, shoes with very striking buckles, a cravat
and jabot of muslin. There emerged from the opening of his collar an Adam's apple that was quite
as prominent as his chin, though it did its best to
escape notice amid the billowing muslin; at the
slightest movement of his jaw his chin made a desperate effort to meet his nose, to which that feature
gallantly responded. One of his eyes remained
hermetically closed; the corner of his mouth and
all the lines of his face were screwed up toward the
other, which shone brightly from behind a shelter-
ing cheekbone and seemed to exclaim: "Beware! I
am here alone, but nothing escapes me!"

Mme de Saint-Auréol was almost entirely hidden in floods of false lace. Her long hands, loaded
with enormous rings, lay nestling and trembling
in the depths of her fluttering sleeves. A kind of
hood made of black taffeta, lined with tatters of
white lace, shrouded her face; it was tied under
her chin with two taffeta strings, which were white
with the powder that fell from her terrifically
painted face. When I came in, she struck an at-

titude in front of me, standing sideways with her head thrown back, and exclaimed in a high, loud, uninflected voice:

"There was a time, sister, when more respect was shown to the name of Saint-Auréol. . . ."

Whom was she attacking? No doubt she wanted to make me feel, and to make her sister feel, that I was not the guest of the Floches'; for she continued, bending her head affectedly to one side, and raising her right hand toward me:

"The Baron and I have much pleasure, monsieur, in receiving you at our table."

I applied my lips to one of her rings and raised my head from the ceremony blushing, for my position between the Saint-Auréols and the Floches threatened to be embarrassing. But Mme Floche appeared to pay no attention to her sister's outburst. As for the Baron, his existence seemed to me problematical, although he was all honey and amiability as far as I was concerned. During the whole of my stay at La Quartfourche, he could not be persuaded to call me anything but M. de Las Cases; which gave him the opportunity of declaring he had met several of my relations at the Tuileries . . . one of my uncles in particular, who used to play piquet with him.

"Ah, he was a queer fellow! Every time he played

a trump, he used to shout out: 'Domino!' . . ."

The Baron's conversation was almost entirely of this caliber. At table he was almost the only person to speak; and then, as soon as the meal was over, he sank into a mummy-like silence.

As we were leaving the dining-room, Mme Floche came up to me and said in a whisper:

"Perhaps you would be so kind, Monsieur Lacase, as to favor me with a few minutes' talk?" A talk that apparently she did not wish anyone to hear, for she began by leading me off in the direction of the kitchen garden, saying out loud that she wanted to show me the espaliers.

"It is about my great-nephew," she began as soon as she was sure we were out of hearing. "I should not like you to think I am criticizing Abbé Santal's teaching . . . but I thought that you, who live in such close proximity to the very fountain-head of learning" (those were her words), "might give us some advice."

"You have only to speak, Madame Floche. I will do whatever I can."

"Well then, for so young a child, I am afraid the subject of his thesis is a little out of the way."

"What thesis?" I asked, feeling slightly at a loss.

"The thesis for his *baccalauréat*." [1]

"Oh, of course," I answered, resolved for the future to be astonished at nothing. "On what subject?"

"Well, Monsieur l'Abbé is afraid that a literary or purely philosophical subject may be too conducive to vagueness in a young mind already over-inclined to daydreaming . . . (that, at least, is what the Abbé says). He has therefore urged Casimir to choose a historical subject."

"A point of view for which there is a great deal to be said. And what is the subject?"

"You must excuse me. I am afraid of mispronouncing the name . . . Averroës."

"The Abbé no doubt had reasons for choosing the subject, which at first sight might seem, it is true, a little peculiar."

"They chose it together. As for the reasons the Abbé put forward, I am quite prepared to endorse them. The anecdotic interest of the subject, he says, is particularly likely to fix Casimir's attention, which is a little given to wandering. And then it has never been treated before, and apparently that is a thing to which the examiners attach the greatest importance."

"I cannot remember, it is true—"

---

[1] An elementary examination, for which no thesis is required.

"And naturally, in order to find a subject that has never been treated before, one has to leave the beaten road."

"Of course!"

"Only, I will tell you what troubles me—but perhaps I am trespassing on your time?"

"Please believe I am most anxious to be of help to you."

"Well, then, it is this. I make no doubt that Casimir will soon be able to pass his thesis fairly brilliantly, but I am afraid that this desire to specialize—this slightly premature desire—may lead the Abbé to neglect his general education a little—arithmetic, for instance, or astronomy."

"And what does Monsieur Floche think about it?" I asked in bewilderment.

"Oh, Monsieur Floche approves of everything the Abbé says or does."

"And the parents?"

"They have put us in charge of the child," said she after a slight hesitation; then, stopping short in her walk:

"As a mark of your kindness, dear Monsieur Lacase, I should be very glad if you would talk to Casimir a little—without seeming actually to question him—and especially not before the Abbé, as he might perhaps take offense. I feel sure that in that way—"

"With the greatest pleasure in the world, madame. I shall certainly have no difficulty in finding some excuse for going out with your nephew. He can show me part of the park."

"He is a little shy at first with people he doesn't know, but he has a confiding nature."

"I have no doubt we shall soon be good friends."

A little later when we were assembled again for tea, "Casimir," said Mme Floche, "you should show Monsieur Lacase the quarry; I am sure it will interest him." Then, coming up to me: "Go quick, before the Abbé comes down, or he will offer to go with you."

I went out into the park at once, while the child, hobbling beside me, pointed out the way.

"I suppose it's recreation time," I began.

He did not answer. I went on:

"Do you never work after tea?"

"Oh, yes; but I have done my copying for the day."

"What is it you copy?"

"The thesis."

"Ah! . . ."

After a little beating about the bush, I succeeded in finding out that this thesis was a work of the Abbé's, which he made the boy, who wrote a good hand, copy out for him. He was making four copies in four cloth-bound copybooks, of which he covered a certain number of pages every day. Casimir declared for that matter that he liked "copying" very much.

"But why four times?"

"Because I don't remember properly."

"Do you understand what you write?"

"Sometimes. Other times the Abbé explains it to me, or else he says I shall understand it when I'm older."

The Abbé had simply turned his pupil into a kind of copying-machine. Was that how he understood his duties? I felt my heart swell with indignation and determined to have a dramatic conversation with him as soon as possible. In my anger I had unconsciously hurried my pace, and Casimir kept up with me with some difficulty; I noticed he was dripping with perspiration. I gave him my hand, which he held in his as he limped along beside me, and at the same time I slackened my pace.

"Is this thesis your only work?"

"Oh, no," said he at once; but when I questioned him further, I understood that he did very little else. He no doubt felt my astonishment.

"I read a great deal," he added, in the kind of voice in which a person in poor circumstances might say: "I have some other clothes."

"And what do you like reading?"

"Travels." Then, looking at me with eyes in which confidence had taken the place of inquiry: "The Abbé has been to China. Did you know?" And his voice expressed boundless admiration—veneration —for his master.

We had now reached the part of the park Mme Floche called the quarry. Long since abandoned, this quarry formed a kind of grotto in the side of the hill, the entrance to which was hidden by bushes. We sat down on a boulder of rock in the warmth of the setting sun. There was no enclosure at this end of the park; on our left hand a path ran slanting downhill and was fenced off by a small railing. Everywhere else the slope of the ground was steep enough to serve as a natural protection.

"And you, Casimir, have you ever traveled?" I asked.

He made no answer and sat with his head down. . . . The little valley at our feet was filling with shade; in front of us the landscape was shut out by a hill, which the rays of the sun had already begun to touch and which was crowned by a clump of oaks and Spanish chestnuts that grew on a chalky mound riddled with the holes of a rabbit-warren. The rather romantic aspect of the place was set off by the uniform softness of the surrounding country.

"Look at the rabbits!" cried Casimir suddenly; then, after a moment, he pointed to the clump of trees and added: "I went up there one day with Monsieur l'Abbé."

On our way home we passed by a pond over-grown with weeds. I promised Casimir to prepare him a line and show him how to fish for frogs.

This first evening of mine, which was brought to a close very little after nine o'clock, differed in no particular from those that followed it, and, I suppose, from those that had preceded it, for my hosts had the good taste not to treat me with any special ceremony. Immediately after dinner we repaired to the drawing-room, where Gratien in the meantime had lighted the fire. A large lamp, placed at one end of a marquetry table, lighted a game of backgammon that the Baron and the Abbé started at the farther end of the table, and a small card-table as well, where the ladies sat down to a lively kind of Oriental bezique.

"Monsieur Lacase, who is accustomed to the dis-sipations of Paris, will no doubt consider our game a little dull . . ." Mme de Saint-Auréol had be-gun by saying.

In the meantime M. Floche dozed in an arm-chair by the fire; Casimir sat plowing his way through a *Round the World*, his elbows on the ta-ble, his head in his hands, his mouth open and slob-

bering. Partly to appear at ease and partly from
politeness, I pretended to take a lively interest in
the ladies' bezique; it could be played like whist
with a dummy, but four made a better game, so
that when I offered to take a hand, Mme de Saint-
Auréol accepted me as a partner with enthusiasm.
The first evening or two, my blunders brought our
side to disaster and were the delight of Mme Floche,
who after every triumph took the liberty of giving
my arm a discreet little tap with her mittened hand.
There were all sorts of openings for boldness, cun-
ning, and finesse. Mlle Olympe played a cautious,
deliberate game. At the beginning of each hand the
players made their stakes and ventured to double
or not according to the cards they held, which gave
a little room for bluff; Mme de Saint-Auréol used
to launch out recklessly, her eyes shining, her cheeks
scarlet, and her chin in a tremble; when she had
a really good hand, she would give me a great kick
under the table; Mlle Olympe did what she could
to stand up to her, but she was completely demoral-
ized by the old lady, who, instead of calling another
number, would suddenly burst out in a shrill voice
with:

"Verdure, that's a lie!"

At the end of the first game Mme Floche would
take out her watch and, as if it were really the exact

hour, "Casimir!" she would call out. "Come, Casimir, it's bedtime."

The boy seemed to wake painfully out of his lethargy, rose, offered the gentlemen his limp hand, the ladies his cheek, and then left the room, dragging his foot behind him.

As Mme de Saint-Auréol invited us to our revenge, the first game of backgammon would come to an end; then M. Floche would sometimes take his brother-in-law's place; neither M. Floche nor the Abbé called their throws, so that nothing was heard from their end but the rattling of the dice in the box and onto the table; M. de Saint-Auréol soliloquized or hummed a tune in the armchair, and sometimes he would smash violently at the fire with the tongs, so recklessly that the red-hot cinders were scattered far and wide; upon which Mlle Olympe would hastily dash to the rescue and perform what Mme de Saint-Auréol elegantly termed "the spark dance" on the carpet. . . . Oftener than not M. Floche left the Abbé to wrestle with the Baron and remained in his armchair; I could see him from my place, not sleeping as he said, but shaking his head in the shadow; and the first evening, when a spurt of flame suddenly lighted his face, I saw that he was crying.

By a quarter past nine the game of bezique was

over, and Mme Floche put out the lamp, while
Mlle Verdure lighted two candelabras, which she
placed on each side of the backgammon board.

"Don't keep him up too long, Abbé," exhorted
Mme de Saint-Auréol, giving her husband's shoulder a tap with her fan.

From the first night on I thought it the proper
thing to obey the ladies' signal and leave the back-
gammon-players to their game and M. Floche, who
was the last to go upstairs, to his meditations. In the
hall everyone took possession of a candle, and the
ladies wished me good-night to the same accompani-
ment of curtsies as in the morning. I went to my
room; soon after, I heard the gentlemen come up.
And soon after that all was quiet. But for a long
time light was to be seen filtering under some of the
doors. And an hour or more later, if for any reason
one had to go into the passage, one ran the risk of
coming upon Mme Floche or Mlle Verdure in night
attire, attending to some last household duty. Later
still, and when one would have thought every light
must be extinguished, a shadow could be seen cast
on the pane of a little closet that had a window opening on the passage but no door,—the shadow of
Mme de Saint-Auréol sitting over her mending.

iv

MY SECOND DAY at La Quartfourche very appreciably resembled the first, even from hour to hour; but any curiosity I may have had concerning the doings of my hosts had now entirely subsided. Ever since morning the rain had been coming down in a steady drizzle. As it was impossible to go out and the ladies' conversation was becoming more and more trifling, I spent practically the whole day over my work. It was all I could do to get a few words with the Abbé after lunch; he invited me to smoke a cigarette with him in a kind of glass house just off the drawing-room, which was called rather pompously "the orangery," where the few seats and chairs used in the garden were stored during the wet weather.

"But, my dear sir," he said, when I tackled him a little nervously on the subject of the boy's education, "I should have been only too glad to give Casimir the benefit of my feeble resources; it was with regret that I gave up the attempt. With that limp of his, would you have suggested my teaching him to dance on the tightrope? I very soon found I had to come down in my aims. If he is studying Averroës with me now, it is because I am engaged in writing a treatise on the philosophy of Aristotle, and rather than keep droning on with the child over the rudiments of spelling or what not, I took a heartfelt pleasure in associating him with my own work. It is as good a subject as any other; the important thing is to keep Casimir busy for three or four hours during the day. Surely some feeling of irritation would have been unavoidable if I had had to waste an equal amount of my own time? And with no profit to him, I assure you. Enough on this subject now, don't you think?" Upon which, throwing away his unfinished cigarette, he got up and returned to the drawing-room.

The bad weather prevented me from going out with Casimir, and we had to put off the proposed fishing expedition till next day; but to make up for the child's disappointment I racked my brains to find some other amusement for him. Finally I managed to get hold of a chessboard and taught him how to play "fox and geese," which game engrossed him till supper time.

The evening began in exactly the same way as the day before, but I had already given up looking at or listening to anybody; a feeling of unspeakable boredom had begun to weigh me down.

Directly after dinner a kind of squall came up. Twice over Mlle Verdure interrupted the bezique to see whether the rain was "driving" into the upstairs rooms. We had to play the return match without her; there was no spirit in it whatever. By the fire, in a low chair, generally spoken of as the *"berline,"* M. Floche, lulled by the sound of the downpour, had actually fallen asleep, while the Baron, sitting opposite him in the *bergère,* groaned and grunted over his rheumatism.

"A game of backgammon would take your thoughts off," the Abbé kept repeating in vain; finally, however, seeing there was no hope of an adversary, he went off to bed, taking Casimir with him.

When, that evening, I found myself once more alone in my room, I was assailed, body and soul, by a feeling of intolerable wretchedness—an ennui so great that it almost took the shape of fear. Here I was, separated from all the rest of the world by a wall of rain, remote from all passion, remote from life, imprisoned in a dreary nightmare among a set of strange beings, scarcely to be called human— cold-blooded, colorless creatures whose hearts had long since ceased to beat. I opened my bag and snatched up my railway timetable. A train! No matter the time, day or night—oh, for a train to carry me away! This is stifling me. . . .

Impatience prevented me from sleeping for a long while.

When I awoke the next morning, though my determination was perhaps no less fixed, yet I felt it impossible to be so lacking in courtesy to my hosts as to go off without inventing some excuse for curtailing my visit so suddenly. I had actually been rash enough to talk of staying at least a week at La Quartfourche! Well, what of it? I must receive some bad news summoning me back to Paris. . . . Fortunately, I had left my address behind me, with directions for my letters to be forwarded to La Quartfourche; it would really be a miracle, I thought, if I did not get some kind of envelope that very day which, with a little skill, would serve my turn . . . and all my hope was fixed on the arrival of the postman. He generally appeared shortly after twelve, while we were finishing lunch; before we left the table, Delphine would bring in the meager little packet of letters and papers, which she took to Mme Floche, who then distributed them to the rest of the party. It happened that day unfortunately that the Abbé Santal had been invited to lunch by the priest of Pont-l'Évêque, and at

about eleven he had come to take leave of M. Floche
and me. It did not strike me at the time that he was
doing me out of the horse and trap.

So at lunch I went through the little performance
I had prepared beforehand.

"Dear, dear! How tiresome!" I murmured as I
opened one of the envelopes handed me by Mme
Floche; and as my hosts tactfully refrained from
noticing this exclamation, I began again rather
more emphatically: "What a piece of bad luck!"
acting surprise and dismay as I gazed at a perfectly
inoffensive note. At last Mme Floche ventured to
ask timidly:

"No bad news, I hope?"

"Oh, nothing really serious," I replied at once,
"but what puts me out is that I see I shall have to
return to Paris immediately."

The consternation from one end of the table to
the other was general and so much greater than I
had expected that I felt myself blushing in confusion. It showed itself, to begin with, in a melancholy silence; then at last M. Floche said in rather
a shaky voice:

"Do you really mean it, my dear young friend?
But your work! But our—"

He was unable to finish. I could think of nothing
to say, nothing to answer, and, upon my word, was

not a little upset myself. My eyes were fixed on the
top of Casimir's head; he, with his nose in his plate,
went on chopping an apple into little bits. Mademoiselle Verdure had turned scarlet with indignation.

"I hardly like to press you to stay," hazarded
Mme Floche feebly.

"For any inducement La Quartfourche may have
to offer!" Mme de Saint-Auréol added acidly.

"Oh, dear lady, believe me, nothing—" I was
beginning to expostulate, but without attending to
me, she shouted into the ear of her husband, who
was sitting next her:

"Monsieur Lacase wants to leave us!"

"Delightful! Delightful! Most kind," said the
deaf man, smiling at me.

In the meantime Mme Floche was consulting
Mlle Verdure:

"But how shall we manage—and the mare just
gone with the Abbé?"

I here conceded a trifle:

"As long as I get to Paris the first thing tomorrow morning. . . . I could make the evening train
do."

"Let Gratien go at once to see if we can have
Bouligny's horse. Say it will be wanted to catch

the—" then, turning to me: "will the seven o'clock
do?"

"Oh, Madame Floche, I am truly sorry to be
giving you so much trouble."

Lunch came to an end in silence. Immediately
afterward little M. Floche carried me off, and as
soon as we were alone in the passage leading to the
library, he began:

"But, my dear sir—my dear friend—I can't yet
believe—but you still have to go through a pile of—
Is it really possible? What a piece of ill luck! What
a sad piece of ill luck! And I was just waiting till
you had finished this first piece of work before hand-
ing over to you some other papers I had got out
last night. I was counting on them, I must confess,
to give you a fresh interest and keep you with us
a little longer. Well, I shall have to let you see them
at once. Come along; you still have some time before evening—for I suppose I mustn't ask you to
come back again?"

The old man's concern made me feel ashamed of
myself. I had been hard at it all the previous day
and the whole of the morning, so that in reality
there was not much left for me to glean from the
first papers confided to me by M. Floche; but as
soon as we had got up into his retreat he proceeded

to pull open a drawer, from the recesses of which
he mysteriously extracted a packet wrapped in linen
and tied up with string into which was slipped a
docket, bearing the descriptions and sources of the
papers to serve as index.

"Take the whole packet," he said; "I dare say it's
not all of it worth much, but you will be able to
sort out whatever is likely to interest you quicker
than I should."

While he was busy again, opening and shutting
one drawer after another, I went down into the
library and spread the bundle out on the big table.

Some of the papers certainly did bear on the subject of my work, but there were not many of them
and they were of little importance. The greater number, in M. Floche's own handwriting, dealt with
the life of Massillon and were consequently of no
use to me.

Could this really have been what poor old Floche
had relied on to keep me at La Quartfourche? I
looked at him; he had now sunk back into his foot-
muff and was engaged with a pin in carefully cleaning out the holes of a little kind of pepperbox that
he used for sprinkling sandarac [1] on his paper. This

---

[1] A kind of resinous gum, which, when reduced to powder, was
used by M. Floche and his contemporaries to sprinkle over
writing-paper in order to prevent it from becoming spongy after
words had been erased by a penknife.

operation over, he raised his head and met my eyes. Such a friendly smile illuminated his countenance that I got up to have a chat with him.

"Monsieur Floche," said I, as I leaned on the lintel at the entrance to his little sanctum, "why do you never come to Paris? We should all be so delighted to see you there."

"At my age moving is difficult and expensive."

"And you don't miss town too much?"

"Bah!" he said, throwing up his hands, "I was prepared to miss it more than I did. Just at first the solitude of the country does seem rather hard to anyone who loves talking; but one gets accustomed to it."

"Then it was not from inclination that you came to live at La Quartfourche?"

He disentangled himself from his foot-muff, stood up, and, putting his hand familiarly on my sleeve, said:

"I had a few colleagues at the Institute for whom I felt some affection, and among them your dear master, Albert Desnos; I really think I was in a fair way to take my place among them. . . ."

It seemed as if he wished to add something, but I did not venture to put a too direct question:

"Was it Madame Floche who was so much attracted by the country?"

"N—o. Still it was on Madame Floche's account I came; but she herself was summoned here by a little family occurrence."

He had come down into the large room and caught sight of the packet, which I had already tied up again.

"Ah, you have been through it already," he said sadly. "Doubtless there was not much you could make use of. Well, well, there it is! I pick up the very smallest crumbs, I know; sometimes I tell myself I am wasting my time gathering straws. But people like myself are needed for these trifling labors, so as to spare others like you who will be able to turn them to brilliant account. It will give me the greatest pleasure, as I read your thesis, to feel that the pains I took may have been of just a little use to you."

Just then the bell summoned us to tea.

How was I to discover, thought I, what this "little family occurrence" could be that had been important enough to make these two old people take such a decision? Did the Abbé know it? Instead of setting myself against him, I should have tried to get round him. It couldn't be helped! It was too late now. All the same, M. Floche was a worthy man whom I should always remember kindly.

"Casimir doesn't dare to ask," said Mme Floche

as we entered the dining-room, "whether you would take another little turn with him in the garden. It's what he would very much like, I know, but perhaps you haven't time."

The child was choking over his cup of milk.

"I was just going to suggest it," I answered; "I have managed to get even with my work and I shall be free now till it's time to start. It seems to have stopped raining too, I see." And I took him off with me into the park.

At the first turn in the path the child, who was holding one of my hands in both his, pressed it against his burning cheek and kept it there.

"You said you were going to stay a week."

"My dear little fellow, I can't stay any longer."

"You're bored."

"No, but I have to go."

"Where are you going?"

"To Paris. But I shall come back again."

He looked anxiously at me as I said the words.

"Really and truly? Do you promise?"

The child's question was so trustful I had not the heart to retract.

"Would you like me to write it on a bit of paper for you to keep?"

"Oh yes!" he exclaimed, kissing my hand with fervor and taking frantic leaps to show his delight.

"And now do you know what I think would be very nice? Instead of going fishing, suppose we were to pick some flowers for your aunt. Then you and I could take a big bouquet into her room as a surprise for her."

I had vowed to myself not to leave La Quart-fourche without having been into the room of one or other of the two old ladies; as they were continually going up and down stairs all over the house, I ran a great risk of being disturbed in my indiscreet investigations; I relied now on the boy as an excuse for my presence. However strange it might appear for me to follow him into his grandmother's or aunt's room, the bouquet would be a good enough pretext to keep me in countenance in case of a surprise.

But picking flowers at La Quartfourche was not so easy as I had supposed. Gratien kept a most suspicious eye on the whole garden; he not only pointed out what flowers it was permissible to pick, but was jealously particular about the way in which they were picked. One had to take pruning-scissors or a knife, and such precautions! This was all explained to me by Casimir. Gratien accompanied us to a bed of magnificent dahlias from which bouquets without number might have been taken and never missed.

"Above the bud, Master Casimir; how many times must you be told? Always cut above the bud."

"At the end of the season like this it's not of the slightest importance," I cried impatiently.

"It's always important," he growled in reply, and "there's never a season for doing wrong."

I can't stand these sententious grumblers. . . .

The child went ahead of me carrying the flowers. As we passed through the hall, I possessed myself of a vase. . . .

A deep religious peace filled the room; the shutters were closed; near the bed, in the depths of an alcove and at the foot of a little crucifix of ivory and ebony, stood a mahogany prie-Dieu covered with dark red velvet. Across the crucifix, and half concealing it, lay a small sprig of box hanging from a pink ribbon and fastened to one arm of the cross. The quiet solemnity of the hour came like a call to prayer. Forgetting what I had come for and the vain curiosity that had brought me to the spot, I left Casimir to arrange the flowers according to his fancy on a chest of drawers, and looked at nothing more in the room. "It is here, then," I thought, "in this great bed, that good old Madame Floche will soon be ending her quiet days, sheltered from every breath of life. . . . O ships questing for storms, how tranquil a haven is this!"

In the meantime Casimir was getting impatient
with his flowers; the heavy-headed dahlias had been
too much for him and the whole bouquet had top-
pled to the floor.

"Come and help me," said he at last.

But when I took his place and began strug-
gling with the flowers, he ran across to a bureau
at the other end of the room and opened it.

"I'm going to write the promise for you to sign
about coming back," he said.

"That's right," I replied, still keeping up my little piece of humbug. "Be quick, though; your aunt
might be cross if she saw you fumbling about in
her writing-table."

"Oh, my aunt's in the kitchen; besides, she never
scolds me."

In the most painstaking fashion he covered a
piece of notepaper with his handwriting.

"Now come and sign."

I went over to the writing-table.

"But Casimir," I said, laughing, "there's no need
for *you* to sign too!" The child, no doubt in order
to make the engagement more binding and to give
himself the impression that he too was pledging
his word, had thought proper to put his own name
at the bottom of the paper, on which I read:

*Monsieur Lacase promises to come back to
La Quartfourche next year.*

                              Casimir de Saint-Auréol

My laughter and comment disconcerted him for
a moment; he himself had taken the whole thing
so seriously to heart! Was it possible that I was
not in earnest? He was on the verge of tears.

"Make room, then," I said, "and let me sign."

He got up and, when I had signed the paper,
jumped for joy and covered my hand with kisses.
Then, just as I was on the point of leaving, he
caught hold of my sleeve and bent over the writing-
table once more.

"I'll show you something," he said, pressing a
spring and sliding out a drawer of which he knew
the secret; then, after groping about a little among
old bills and scraps of ribbon, he held out to me
a delicately framed miniature.

"Look!"

I took it to the window.

In what fairy story is it that the prince falls in
love with the princess's portrait without having seen
her? This must have been the very portrait. I know
nothing about painting and take little interest in
its technical qualities; no doubt a connoisseur would
have pronounced the miniature affected: character

had been almost obliterated by a too flattering insistence on grace; but the grace was there, and so pure and perfect as to be unforgettable.

I cared very little, as I have said, about the good or bad points of the painting: the young woman I had before me showed her profile only; one temple half hidden by a heavy dark curl; a languid eye, dreamy and melancholy; half-opened lips, as if just parted in a sigh, and a slender neck, fragile as the stem of a flower. It was a face of the most disturbing, the most angelic beauty. I lost all consciousness of hour and place as I gazed at it. Casimir, who had left me to put the finishing touches to the flowers, came back and bent over the portrait.

"That's Mamma. Isn't she pretty?"

I felt almost ashamed in the child's presence to think his mother so beautiful.

"Where is your mamma now?"

"I don't know."

"Why isn't she here?"

"She's bored here."

"And your father?"

He hung his head, a little confused and shamefaced, and answered:

"My father is dead."

My questions made him uncomfortable, but I was determined to go on.

"I suppose your mamma comes to see you sometimes?"

"Oh, yes, often!" he replied with conviction, and
raised his head quickly. Then he added in a lower
voice:

"She comes to talk to my aunt."

"But doesn't she talk to you too?"

"Oh, I can't talk to her . . . and besides I'm in
bed when she comes."

"In bed!"

"Yes, she comes at night. . . ." Then his trust-
fulness got the better of him (I had put down the
portrait and he had taken hold of my hand) and
he added tenderly and almost as if it were a secret:

"Last time she came and kissed me in bed."

"Then doesn't she generally kiss you?"

"Oh yes, often."

"Then why do you say 'last time'?"

"Because she was crying."

"Was she with your aunt?"

"No, she came in all by herself in the dark. She
thought I was asleep."

"Did she wake you up?"

"Oh, I wasn't asleep. I was waiting till she came."

"You knew she was there, then?"

He looked down again without answering. I insisted:

"How did you know she was there?"

No answer. I still went on:

"How could you see she was crying in the dark?"

"Oh, I could feel it."

"Didn't you ask her to stay?"

"Oh, yes, I did. She was bending over my bed; I took hold of her hair. . . ."

"And what did she say?"

"She laughed. She said I was disarranging her hair—but that she had to go."

"Then she doesn't love you?"

"Oh yes, she loves me very much," he cried, so passionately and with such a scarlet face, as he drew abruptly back from my side, that I felt ashamed of my question.

Mme Floche's voice was heard calling from the foot of the stairs:

"Casimir! Casimir! Go and tell Monsieur Lacase that it's time for him to get ready. The carriage will be here in half an hour."

I sprang up and dashed downstairs to where the old lady was standing in the hall.

"Madame Floche!" I cried, "is there anyone who could take a telegram for me? I have thought of a plan that I believe will let me stay a few more days with you."

She took me by both hands.

"Oh, dear Monsieur Lacase, how very unlikely!"
And as, in her emotion, she could think of nothing
else to say, she kept on repeating: "How very unlikely!" . . . At last, running out, she called up to
M. Floche's window: "Good man! Good man!"
(that was what she called him). "Monsieur Lacase
has consented to stay."

Her feeble voice, shrill and cracked though it
was, succeeded in reaching him; I saw the window
open, M. Floche looked out for a moment, and as
soon as he understood the situation called to me:

"I'll come down! I'll come down!"

Casimir joined him and for several minutes I had
to confront their joint congratulations; I might have
been one of the family.

I wrote some kind of fantastic message by way
of telegram and had it dispatched to an imaginary
address.

"I'm afraid," said Mme Floche, "I was a little indiscreet at lunch and pressed you too much to stay.
I hope, if you do, your affairs in Paris won't suffer?"

"I hope not, dear lady; I have asked a friend to
see to them for me."

Mme de Saint-Auréol now appeared on the scene.
She walked round the room, fanning herself and
screaming in her most piercing tones: "Now, that's
very kind of him! A thousand thanks! . . . How

kind!" Then she disappeared and all was calm
again.

Shortly before dinner the Abbé returned from
Pont-l'Évêque; as he had not heard of my intended
departure, he could not be surprised to learn I was
remaining.

"Monsieur Lacase," he said quite affably, "I have
brought you back a few papers from Pont-l'Évêque;
I am not myself very fond of newspaper gossip, but
I thought you must be a little lacking in news here
and might care to see them."

He felt about in his cassock for them. "Dear me!
Gratien must have taken them up to my room with
my bag. Wait a moment; I'll go and get them."

"Please don't trouble, Monsieur l'Abbé," I said;
"I will come for them myself."

I went up to his room with him and he invited
me to come in. While he was brushing his cassock
and getting ready for dinner, I asked him, after
a few casual remarks, whether he had known the
Saint-Auréols before coming to La Quartfourche.

"No," he said.

"Nor Monsieur Floche?"

"I suddenly left mission work to take up teaching. My Superior had been in communication with
Monsieur Floche and he appointed me to the post

I now occupy. No, before coming here I knew
neither my pupil nor any of his family."

"So that you don't know what caused Monsieur
Floche to leave Paris so suddenly fifteen years ago,
just as he was going to become a member of the
Institute?"

"Money troubles," he grunted.

"What! Then are Monsieur and Madame Floche
living here as dependents of the Saint-Auréols?"

"Not at all, not at all!" he exclaimed impatiently;
"it is the Saint-Auréols who are ruined, or almost
so. All the same, La Quartfourche belongs to them,
and the Floches, who are comfortably off, live with
them in order to help things out; they assist in running the house and make it possible for the Saint-
Auréols to keep La Quartfourche, which will eventually go to Casimir. That's about all, I think, the
child can hope for. . . ."

"Then the daughter-in-law has no money?"

"What daughter-in-law? Casimir's mother is not
the daughter-in-law. She is the Saint-Auréols' own
daughter."

"But then what about the child's name?" He pretended not to understand me. "Isn't he called Casimir de Saint-Auréol?"

"Really!" he said ironically. "Then it is to be

supposed that Mademoiselle de Saint-Auréol must have married some cousin of the same name."

"Oh, very well," I said, half taking his meaning and yet hesitating to draw the conclusion. He had finished brushing his cassock and, with his foot on the window-sill, was busily flicking the dust from his shoes with a handkerchief. "And do you know her—this Mademoiselle de Saint-Auréol?"

"I have seen her two or three times, but she only pays flying visits here."

"Where does she live?"

He straightened himself, flung the dusty handkerchief into a corner of the room, and exclaimed:

"So it's an inquisition, is it?" Then, going toward his washstand: "The dinner bell will be ringing in a minute and I shan't be ready."

It was a plain invitation for me to leave him; his pursed-up lips, I felt sure, had a deal to say, but for the moment they would let nothing more escape them.

v

FOUR DAYS LATER I was still at La Quartfourche, suffering less from the horrid tedium of the third day, but more from fatigue. I had discovered nothing new, either from the events of each day or from my hosts' conversation. I felt my curiosity to be already dying of inanition. "I see I must give up trying to find out anything fresh," I thought as I once more set about preparing for my departure: "I am cut off from information on all sides; the Abbé appears to have been struck dumb ever since I have let him see how much interested I am in what he knows; the more confiding Casimir becomes, the more constrained I feel with him; I dare not question him further and besides I now know all he can tell me—nothing more than on the day he showed me the portrait."

Yes, one thing; the boy had very innocently let fall his mother's name. No doubt I was mad to work myself up into such a state over a flattering picture, which in all likelihood was more than fifteen years old; and even if Isabelle de Saint-Auréol were to venture on one of her fugitive appearances while I was still staying at La Quartfourche, I should probably not have the power, or the courage, to put myself in her way. No matter! My thoughts had suddenly become so full of her that all my depression of spirits vanished; the last days had fled by on wings and I was astonished to find myself already at the end of the week. It had never been suggested I should stay longer at the Floches' and my work gave me no excuse for further delay, but now that the last morning had come, I spent it wandering about the park, which autumn had made more spacious and sonorous, calling upon the name of Isabelle, below my breath at first, and then aloud: "Isabelle! . . ." and the name, which I had disliked at first, seemed now to be fraught with elegance and rich with some clandestine charm. . . . Isabelle de Saint-Auréol! Isabelle! I saw her white dress flit before me round every turning of the path; every gleam of light that shone through the wavering foliage recalled her glance, her melancholy smile; and because as yet I knew nothing of love, I fancied I was in love and indulged myself in that delightful idea.

Oh, how beautiful the park was! How nobly it prepared to welcome the melancholy of the declin-

ing season! I inhaled with rapture the smell of the
dank moss and rotting leaves. The great chestnut
trees, whose branches swept the ground, were red
and half stripped already of their leaves; some of
the bushes glowed through the rain with a crimson
fire; beside them the grass took on a more vivid
green; a few autumn crocuses showed on the garden
lawns, and lower down, in the little valley, a field
was pink with them—one could see it from the
quarry, where, when the rain stopped, I used to go
and sit sometimes, on the same stone where I had
sat with Casimir the first day—where perhaps Mlle
de Saint-Auréol herself had once sat and dreamed
. . . and I imagined myself sitting beside her.

Casimir used often to come with me, but I preferred walking by myself. Nearly every day I was
caught by rain in the garden; I used to go in dripping and dry myself by the kitchen fire. Neither
the cook nor Gratien liked me; my repeated ad-
vances had not succeeded in extracting half a dozen
words from them. I had not been able to make
friends with the dog either, however much I patted
him or fed him with titbits; Terno spent almost the
whole day lying in the huge fireplace and whenever
I came near, he growled. Casimir, whom I often
used to find sitting on the edge of the hearthstone,
peeling vegetables or reading, was distressed that

his dog refused to treat me as a friend and would give him a reproving tap. I used often to take the book from the boy's hands and go on reading it aloud to him; he would lean up against me and I felt him listening with his whole body.

But on this particular morning the shower that caught me was so sudden and violent that it was impossible to think of getting back to the château; I ran to the nearest shelter; it was the deserted lodge you may have seen at the other end of the park near the gates; even then it was dilapidated; the rather large first room, however, was still elegantly paneled, like the drawing-room of a pleasure-lodge; but the woodwork was worm-eaten and broke away at the slightest touch. . . .

When I pushed open the badly fitting door and went in, a number of bats fluttered round and then flew out of the unglazed window. I had thought it was only a passing shower, but while I stood waiting with what patience I could, the sky darkened and became completely overcast. Here I was a prisoner, then, and no doubt for some time to come! It was half past ten; lunch was not till twelve. I made up my mind to wait for the first bell, which I thought I should be sure to hear from where I was; I had writing materials with me, and as I was behindhand with my correspondence, I proposed to

prove to myself that an hour might be as well spent
as a day. But my thoughts constantly flew back to
the object of my anxious hopes and fears: oh, if I
could only believe that this place would ever see
her again, I would set the walls ablaze with passionate declarations! . . . And then a mortal ennui, heavy with tears, slowly overwhelmed me. I
sank down on the floor in a corner of the room, for
there was nothing in the way of a seat, and wept
like a lost child.

The word *ennui* is doubtless too weak to describe
the fits of intolerable depression to which I have
been subject ever since I can remember; they overcome one suddenly; something indefinable in the air
starts them; a second before, all was smiling, all was
enjoyable; suddenly a murky vapor rises from the
depths of the soul and interposes itself between desire and life; it forms a kind of livid screen that
separates us from the rest of the world, whose
warmth, love, color, and harmony can now only
reach us as a refracted, warped, transposed abstrac-
tion; we are aware of things, but they fail to move
us, and the desperate effort to break through the
screen that thus isolates our soul, might well lead
us into any sort of crime—murder or suicide, or
madness. . . .

So I dreamed as I listened to the pouring of

the rain. I was holding in my hand the penknife I had opened in order to sharpen my pencil, but the paper in my notebook still remained a blank; and with the point of my knife I began to carve her name on a panel near by, not with much conviction, but because I knew such was the habit of all fond lovers; the wood was so rotten, however, that it kept breaking away and a hole would appear instead of the letter; I soon ceased to take any trouble; in mere idleness, with a foolish desire for destruction, I began slashing at random. The panel I was thus spoiling happened to be immediately under the window; the upper part had come away from its framework, so that the whole panel was able to slide upwards in the side grooves. This became evident when the pressure of my knife unexpectedly lifted it.

In a few moments I had finished hacking the panel to pieces. Among the litter of wood there fell to the ground an envelope; it was so stained and so moldy, so much the color of the wall, that at first it gave me no shock of astonishment; no, I was not astonished to see it; I did not think it surprising it should be there, and so great was my apathy that at first I made no attempt to open it. Ugly, gray, dirty, I assure you that it looked like nothing but a flake of plaster. I took it up idly; mechanically I

tore it open. I pulled out two sheets covered with
a large irregular, faded handwriting, which in places,
indeed, had all but disappeared. What was this letter doing here? I looked at the signature and my
brain reeled: at the bottom of those pages stood the
name of Isabelle!

My thoughts were so full of her . . . for a moment I was under the illusion that it was to me she
was writing:

My love, this is my last letter [she began].
*Just these few words more in haste, for tonight I
know I shall be unable to speak; my lips, so close
to yours, will find no words but kisses. Quickly,
while it is still possible, listen.*

*Eleven o'clock is too early; twelve will be
better. You know I am dying of impatience and
that waiting kills me, but we must be sure the others
are asleep before I can at last waken to be yours.
Yes, midnight; not before. Come to the kitchen
door to meet me (you must follow the wall of the
kitchen garden, where you will be in the shadow—
after that, there are some bushes), wait for me there
and not at the park gates, not that I am afraid of
crossing the garden by myself, but the bag I shall
be taking for a few clothes will be heavy and I am
not strong enough to carry it far.*

And besides it will be better for the carriage to wait at the bottom of the lane, where we shall find it easily. And wiser, because the farm dogs might bark and give the alarm.

No, dear love, it was impossible, you know very well, for us to have met oftener so as to arrange all this by word of mouth. You know I am a prisoner here and the old people do not allow me to go out any more than they let you come in. Ah, what a dungeon I am escaping from! . . . Yes, I will be careful to bring an extra pair of shoes with me and change into them as soon as we are in the carriage, for the grass at the bottom of the garden is sopping.

How can you ask whether I am still resolved and ready? Why, my beloved, for months I have been preparing and holding myself ready! For years I have been living and waiting for this moment! —And whether I shall regret nothing? Don't you understand, then, that I have taken a loathing to everyone here who is attached to me—to everyone and everything that attaches me to this place? Is it really your gentle, timid Isa who speaks so? My dear, my lover, what have you done to me, beloved? . . .

This place is stifling me; I dream of the

*elsewhere that is opening out before me. . . . I
thirst. . . .*

*I was forgetting to say that I have not been
able to take the sapphires out of the case, because
my aunt never leaves the keys in her room now, and
none of those I have tried will unlock the drawer.
Don't scold me; I have got Mamma's bracelet, the
enamel chain, and two rings, which I don't suppose
are very valuable, as she never wears them; but I
think the chain is very fine. As for money, I will do
what I can, but you had better get some too.*

*Yours, with all my prayers. Soon, soon to
meet!*

Your

Isa

*Dated this twenty-second day of October,
my twenty-second birthday and the eve of
my flight.*

I think with terror of all the stuff I should have
to spin out here if I had to cook this story up into
a novel—four or five pages at least of reflections
after reading the letter, interrogations, perplexities. . . . In reality, as after any very violent shock,
I fell into a state of semi-lethargy. When at last,
through the confused rushing of blood in my brain,

I heard the sound of a bell, which was then repeated, "Heavens!" I thought, "it's the second luncheon-bell! How can I have missed hearing the first?" I pulled out my watch. Twelve o'clock! I dashed out instantly with the glowing letter pressed to my heart, and darted back to the house, bareheaded, through the rain.

The Floches were already wondering anxiously what had become of me, and when I appeared, panting, "Why, dear Monsieur Lacase, you are drenched," they cried, "absolutely drenched!"

Then they declared no one should sit down to table until I had changed my clothes; and as soon as I came down they began to question me with kind solicitude; I had to explain that I had taken shelter in the lodge and had waited in vain for a break in the shower; then they apologized for the bad weather, for the shocking state of the paths, for the second bell, which had certainly been rung too soon, for the first, which had not been rung as loud as usual. . . . Mlle Verdure went to fetch a shawl, which they implored me to put round my shoulders, because I was still overheated and might catch cold. The Abbé meanwhile was watching me without saying a word, with his lips screwed up into a regular grimace, and so nervous was I under his searching glance, that I felt myself blush and grow as uneasy

as a child who has been caught in a misdemeanor.
"But it is essential for me to get round him," I
thought, "for he is now the only person from whom
it will be possible to learn anything—the only person who may cast some light on the intricacies of
this dark and mysterious affair, which I am bent on
exploring now more out of love than curiosity."

After coffee the cigarette I offered the Abbé served
as an excuse for a private conversation; we went to
smoke in the orangery, in order not to incommode
the Baronne.

"I thought you were only going to stop here a
week," he began in an ironical voice.

"I was not counting on such kind hosts."

"Then Monsieur Floche's documents—?"

"Are assimilated. . . . But I have found other
things that interest me more."

I expected a question, but none came.

"You must know the secrets of this château inside
out," I went on impatiently.

He opened his eyes wide, wrinkled his brows, and
put on an air of stupid candor.

"Why is Madame, or Mademoiselle, de Saint-
Auréol, your pupil's mother, not here with us, engaged in looking after her afflicted son and her aged
parents?"

In order better to feign astonishment, he threw

away his cigarette and opened his hands in a paren-
thesis on each side of his face.

"No doubt her occupations detain her elsewhere . . ." he muttered. "What an insidious question!"

"Do you want one that is more to the point? What
did Madame or Mademoiselle de Saint-Auréol, your
pupil's mother, do on a certain October 22, the night
fixed for her to run away with her lover?"

He struck an attitude, with his hands on his hips.

"Oho! Oho! my young novelist!" (I had been
vain or weak enough some time previously to con-
fide in him the kind of thing that should never be
spoken of except in cases of deep personal sympathy; and since he had become aware of my proclivi-
ties he had taken to laughing at me in a way I was
beginning to find intolerable.) "Aren't you going a
little fast? . . . And may I ask you in my turn how
you come to know so much?"

"Because the letter Isabelle de Saint-Auréol wrote
to her lover that day did not fall into his hands but
into mine."

Decidedly I was a person to be reckoned with;
just at that moment the Abbé discovered a little spot
on the sleeve of his cassock and began scratching it
with his fingernail; he was coming to terms.

"There is one thing that surprises me," he said,

"that as soon as a person considers himself a born novelist, he thinks he has a right to do anything he pleases. Anybody else would think twice before reading a letter that was not addressed to him."

"I hope, Monsieur l'Abbé, he would not read it at all."

I looked at him steadily, but he kept on scratching with his eyes down.

"I hardly suppose though that anyone gave it to you to read."

"The letter fell into my hands accidentally; the envelope was old, dirty, half torn, and without a trace of writing on it; when I opened it, I saw it was a letter from Mademoiselle de Saint-Auréol; but addressed to whom? . . . Come now, Monsieur l'Abbé, help me: who was Mademoiselle de Saint-Auréol's lover fourteen years ago?"

The Abbé had risen; he began to walk up and down, his head lowered, his hands crossed behind his back; as he passed behind my chair, he stopped; and I suddenly felt his hands alight heavily on my shoulders:

"Show me that letter."

"Will you speak then?"

I felt his grasp quivering with impatience.

"Oh, no conditions, I beg. Show me the letter —that's enough."

"Let me go and get it," I said, trying to free myself.

"You have it there in your pocket."

He fixed his eyes on the right spot, as if my coat had been transparent. Hang it all! He could hardly be going to search me! . . .

I was in a very bad posture for defending myself, and against a great strapping fellow too, who was stronger than I; and what means should I have afterward of making him speak? I turned round and saw his face almost touching mine—a swollen, red, apoplectic face, with two great veins starting out on the forehead and ugly pockets under the eyes. Then, forcing myself to laugh, for fear of things going altogether wrong:

"Gracious goodness, Abbé, you must confess you know something of curiosity yourself!"

He let go his hold; I rose at once and made as though to leave the room.

"If you had not behaved yourself so like a brigand, I should have shown it to you long ago." Then, taking his arm: "But let's go nearer the drawing-room, so that I may call for help if necessary."

By a great effort of will I kept up a joking manner, but my heart was beating fast.

"There! Read it before me," I said, taking the letter from my pocket. "I want to see what kind of face an Abbé makes when he reads a love-letter."

But he had recovered control of himself and only
showed his agitation by the irrepressible twitching
of a little muscle in his cheek. He read the letter,
then smelt the paper, frowning severely as he
sniffed, so that his eyes seemed to be reproving the
greediness of his nose; then folding the paper up
again, he returned it to me and said somewhat
solemnly:

"On that same 22nd of October, Viscount Blaise
de Gonfreville perished in a hunting accident."

"You make my blood run cold!" (My imagination at once built up an appalling drama.) "You
must know that I found the letter behind a panel
in the lodge, from which place he was certainly
meant to fetch it."

The Abbé then told me that young Gonfreville,
the eldest son of a family whose estate bordered
upon the Saint-Auréols', had been found dead beside a gate he had apparently been intending to
climb, when a clumsy movement had made his gun
go off. No cartridge, however, had been found in
the barrel of his gun. Not a soul could give any
information about the accident; the young man
had gone out alone without being seen by anyone;
but the next day one of the La Quartfourche dogs
had been found licking a pool of blood.

"I was not at La Quartfourche at the time,"

continued he, "but from what I afterward learned, it seems to me certain that the crime was committed by Gratien, who had no doubt discovered his young mistress's relations with the Viscount and had perhaps heard of her proposed flight (which I myself knew nothing of before reading this letter); he is a rough, dogged fellow—vindictive too, perhaps—an old servant who, if it came to the point, might very well think he need stick at nothing in defense of his masters' property."

"Why was he not arrested?"

"It was nobody's interest to prosecute him, and the two families of Gonfrevilles and Saint-Auréols were equally anxious to hush up this unfortunate affair; for a few months later Mademoiselle de Saint-Auréol gave birth to a wretched little child. Casimir's deformity is attributed to the pains his mother took to hide her condition; but God teaches us that the sins of the fathers are often visited on the children. Come with me to the lodge; I am curious to see the place where you found the letter."

The sky had cleared and we set out together.

Everything went smoothly on our way to the lodge; the Abbé took my arm and we walked in step together, talking amicably. But on the way back

it was another matter. No doubt we were both somewhat excited by the strangeness of the adventure;
but each of us in a very different manner. Quickly
disarmed by the smiling and obliging way with
which the Abbé had finally told me what he knew,
I forgot his cloth and my own reserve and found
myself speaking to him as man to man. . . . This,
I think, is how the quarrel began:

"Who will tell us," said I, "what Mademoiselle
de Saint-Auréol did that night? No doubt she didn't
learn of the Count's death until the next day. Did
she wait for him in the garden? And for how long?
What were her thoughts when she saw he was not
coming?"

The Abbé, absolutely unmoved by my psychological flights, remained silent. I went on:

"Think of the delicate young girl, her heart
heavy with love and discontent, her head full of
wild fancies—think of the passionate Isabelle—"

"The shameless Isabelle," muttered the Abbé below his breath.

I continued as if I had not heard him, but in my
growing excitement I was already preparing to answer his next interjection.

"Think," I exclaimed, "of all the hope and all
the despair that must—"

"Why think of all that?" he interrupted sharply.

"It is not our business to know more about events than that part of them that may serve to instruct us."

"But according as we know more or less, they will instruct us differently. . . ."

"What do you mean?"

"That the superficial knowledge of events does not always, nor indeed often, concord with the deeper knowledge we may gain of them later, and that the instruction they then bring with them will not be the same; that it is a good thing to inquire before drawing conclusions. . . ."

"Take care, my young friend, take care! There is a germ of revolt lying in the spirit of inquiry and critical curiosity. The great man you have chosen for your model should have shown you—"

"The great man I have chosen to write my thesis on, you mean. . . ."

"What a hairsplitter you are! That is the spirit which—"

"But really, my dear Abbé, I should like to know whether it wasn't that selfsame spirit of curiosity that made you come with me just now to the lodge, that made you hang for several moments over a broken panel, and that has gradually driven you to find out all the details of the story you have just told me! . . ."

His step became more agitated, his voice sharper; he tapped the ground impatiently with his stick.

"I don't look for explanations of explanations like you. I go no farther than the fact itself. The lamentable occurrences I have acquainted you with would teach me, if I still needed teaching, to look on carnal sin with horror; I find here the condemnation of divorce and of all men's contrivances for palliating the consequences of their offenses. That is surely sufficient!"

"No, not for me. I care nothing for the fact so long as I cannot discover its cause. To learn Isabelle de Saint-Auréol's secret life, to trace out the perfumed paths she trod, their pathos, their darkness—"

"Take care, young man! You are falling in love with her!"

"Ah! I was expecting that! Because I am not satisfied with appearances, because words do not blind me, nor acts either— Are you sure you are not judging her unfairly?"

"The trollop!"

I grew hot with indignation. It was with the greatest difficulty that I controlled myself.

"Monsieur l'Abbé, such words surprise me in your mouth. I thought that Christ had taught us to forgive, not to chastise."

"There is but one step from indulgence to encouragement."

"*He* at any rate would not have condemned her as you do."

"In the first place, what do you know about that? In the second place, He who is without sin Himself may show more indulgence toward the sins of others than—I mean it is not the business of us sinners to find more or less excuse for sin, but simply to turn aside from it with horror."

"After having first taken a good sniff at it, as you did at the letter!"

"Impertinence!" And abruptly breaking away from me, he darted off down a little side path, flinging biting words behind him, like Parthian shots; I could make out only a few of them: "Modern education! . . . Sophist! . . . Anarchist! . . ."

When we met again at dinner, he still looked frowningly, but as we left the table, he came up to me with a smile and put out his hand, which I took with a smile too.

The evening seemed to me more dismal even than usual. The Baron groaned softly by the fireside. M. Floche and the Abbé moved their draughts without a word. I saw Casimir out of the corner of my

eye, with his head buried in his hands, slowly slob-
bering onto his book and from time to time mop-
ping it with his handkerchief. I gave only just sufficient attention to the game of bezique to prevent
my partner from being too ignominiously beaten;
Mme Floche noticed my dullness and tried anxiously to make the game a little more lively:

"Now then, Olympe! It's your turn. Are you
asleep?"

No, it was not sleep but death that was benumb-
ing my hosts with its grim and icy touch. I myself
felt a mortal anguish, a kind of horror, seize me.
O spring! O gusts of heaven, perfumes and delights
and aery music, never more will you be wafted
here! So I dreamed; and I thought of you, Isabelle.
What of the tomb you escaped from? What of the
life you fled to? I imagined you sitting there—there,
in the peaceful lamplight, your pale forehead droop-
ing on your delicate fingers, a curl of black hair
touching—caressing—your wrist. What a far-away
look is in your eyes! That sigh the others do not
hear—what nameless weariness of flesh and spirit
does it tell of so plaintively? And I myself unconsciously heaved a huge sigh, which was partly a
yawn and partly a sob, so that Mme de Saint-
Auréol, throwing her last trump on the table, exclaimed:

"I think Monsieur Lacase is badly wanting to go
off to bed."

Poor lady!

That night I had an absurd dream—a dream that
at first was merely a continuation of the reality.

The evening was not over; I was still in the
drawing-room with my hosts, but a set of people
were there too whose numbers were continually in-
creasing, though I never actually saw anyone come
into the room; I recognized Casimir sitting at a
game of patience over which three or four persons
were bending. Everyone was talking in whispers,
so that at first I could not make out any actual
words, but I realized that everyone present was
pointing out something extraordinary to his neighbor, who in his turn showed astonishment; they
were all looking at one particular point, just beside
Casimir, and I suddenly saw that there, at that very
table, was seated—how had I not noticed her before?—Isabelle de Saint-Auréol. She alone, among
all the other persons in dark clothes, was dressed in
white. At first I thought she looked charming, not
unlike her portrait in the locket; but after a moment, I was struck by the immobility of her features, the fixity of her stare, and I suddenly under-

stood what was being whispered all about me: it
was not the real Isabelle who was there, but a doll
got up to look like her, which had been put in her
place during the real one's absence. This doll, I
thought, was frightful; its air of pretentious stu-
pidity got painfully on my nerves; it seemed to be
motionless, but as I looked at it attentively, I saw
it slowly bend over to one side—lower—lower . . .
it was on the point of toppling over, when Mlle
Olympe, rushing up from the other end of the
drawing-room, stooped down to the ground, lifted
the armchair's loose cover, and began winding up
some sort of oddly creaking machinery which
righted the figure again, and at the same time set
its arms working with the grotesque gestures of
an automaton. Everyone then got up, the hour for
departure having struck; the false Isabelle was to
be left there by herself; on going out everyone
saluted her with a Turkish salaam, except the
Baron, who went up to her and, irreverently seizing her wig with his hand, planted two smacking
kisses on her sinciput, chuckling as he did so. As
soon as the company had all left the drawing-room
—and I saw crowds go out—as soon as it was quite
dark, I saw—yes, in the dark—I saw the doll turn
pale, quiver, come to life. She rose slowly and it was
Mlle de Saint-Auréol herself; she glided toward

me noiselessly; suddenly I felt her soft arms round my neck, and I woke up in the warm moisture of her breath, just as she was saying tenderly:

"For all the others I am absent—for you only do I come."

I am neither superstitious nor nervous; if I lighted my candle, it was in order to banish this haunting image from my eyes and mind; I found it difficult. In spite of myself, I listened to every sound. Suppose she were really to come! In vain I endeavored to read; I could fix my attention on nothing else; I was still thinking of her when in the early morning I fell asleep.

vi

AND SO THE ups and downs of my lovesick curiosity flared and flickered. It was impossible, however, to put off my departure—which I had again announced—any longer, and this was my last day at La Quartfourche. It was on this day that—

Imagine us sitting at lunch, waiting for the mail, which Gratien's wife, Delphine, usually brings in a little before dessert. It is first taken, as I have said before, to Mme Floche, who sorts out the letters and hands M. Floche the *Journal des Débats*, behind which he disappears until we leave the table. This morning a mauve envelope, which has accidentally caught in the wrapper of the paper, suddenly drops out and flies across the table toward Mme Floche's plate. I have just time to recognize the large straggling writing, which had already made my heart beat the day before. Mme Floche apparently recognizes it too; she makes a hasty effort to cover the envelope with her plate; the plate knocks against a glass and breaks it, spilling the

wine all over the tablecloth. In the turmoil that follows, good Mme Floche, taking advantage of the
general confusion, succeeds in spiriting away the
envelope and concealing it under her mitten.

"I was trying to kill a spider," she says awkwardly, like a child excusing herself. (Whatever
insect happens to come out of the fruit dishes, she
always calls a spider—it is no matter to her whether
it is really a woodlouse or an earwig.)

"And I'll wager you missed it," says Mme de
Saint-Auréol acidly, getting up and throwing her
napkin on the table unfolded. "Please come to me
in the drawing-room, sister. The gentlemen will excuse me; I've got my stomach cramps again."

The meal comes to an end in silence. M. Floche
has seen nothing, and M. de Saint-Auréol understood nothing. Mlle Verdure and the Abbé sit with
their eyes fixed on their plates; if Casimir weren't
blowing his nose, I should think he was crying. . . .

The weather is almost warm, and coffee is served
on the little terrace outside the drawing-room windows. I am the only person to take it with Mlle Verdure and the Abbé; from the drawing-room, where
the two ladies are shut up together, can be heard an
occasional outburst of voices; then silence; the ladies have gone upstairs.

It was at this moment, if I remember right, that the engagement of the parsley-leaved beech took place.

Mlle Verdure and the Abbé lived in a continual state of warfare. Their battles were not very serious and merely amused the Abbé; nothing, however, irritated Mlle Verdure more than the derisive tone adopted by him on these occasions; she came out into the open at every shot and the Abbé fired his volleys point-blank. Hardly a day passed without one of these skirmishes, referred to by the Abbé as "engagements." He used to declare they were good for the old maid's health and he would set to work to get a rise out of her just as one takes a dog out for a walk. It was done perhaps without unkindness, but certainly not without a spice of malice, and he could be not a little provoking. It gave them both something to do and added a flavor to their day.

We had all been somewhat upset by the little incident at dessert and I cast about in search of some diversion. While the Abbé was pouring out the coffee, I put my hand into my pocket and came upon a little bunch of leaves—a twig I had that morning broken off a curious tree that grew by the park gate. I had meant to ask Mlle Verdure its name, not so much out of curiosity to know it as because it flattered her to have an appeal made to her learning.

For she loved botanizing. Now and then she would start out for the day to collect specimens, looking somewhat absurd, with a green box slung across her sturdy shoulders; and all the hours she could spare from her domestic cares were divided between her dried plants and her magnifying glass. . . . Mlle Olympe, therefore, took the twig and without a moment's hesitation pronounced it to be parsley-leaved beech.

"What a queer name!" said I doubtfully; "one can hardly imagine these lanceolate leaves having any connection with—"

The Abbé, who had been smiling significantly for the last minute or two, now observed carelessly:

"That is the name they give the *Fagus persicifolia* at La Quartfourche."

Mlle Verdure positively jumped.

"I didn't know you were so good at botany," she said.

"No, perhaps not," he said, "but I happen to know a little Latin." He turned to me. "These ladies are the victims of an unintentional pun. *Persicus*, my dear lady," he went on, "*persicus* means

peach tree, not *parsley*.[1] The *Fagus persicifolia*,
whose leaves Monsieur Lacase has noticed and so
correctly called lanceolate—the *Fagus persicifolia*
is a *peach*-leaved beech tree."

Mlle Olympe had turned crimson; the affected
unconcern of the Abbé put the final touch to her
discomfiture.

"True botany has nothing to do with anomalies
and monstrosities," was all she managed to get out,
and without another look at the Abbé she emptied
her cup at one gulp and flounced off.

The Abbé had screwed up his mouth till it looked
like the hinder end of a hen and was letting off a
series of small explosions. It was with the greatest
difficulty that I kept from laughing.

"Monsieur l'Abbé," I said, "I'm afraid you're a
wicked man!"

"Not at all! Not at all! . . . The good lady
doesn't take enough exercise; she wants stirring
up now and then. She's very pugnacious, believe
me; if I let her go three days without a taste of
my steel, she comes thrusting at me herself. There
are not so many amusements at La Quartfourche,
you know!"

And then, without a word being said on either

---

[1] *Persil* in French.

side, we both began to think of the letter at the luncheon table.

"Did you recognize the handwriting?" I ventured to ask at last.

He shrugged his shoulders. "A little sooner or a little later, it's the letter that comes to La Quartfourche twice a year, after rent-day, in which she announces her arrival to Madame Floche."

"She is coming, then?" I cried.

"Now, now, keep calm; you won't see her."

"And why shouldn't I see her?"

"Because she arrives in the middle of the night and goes away again almost at once, because she doesn't want to be seen by anyone, and—beware of Gratien."

He gave me a searching look, but I did not move a muscle and he continued with some irritation:

"You won't pay any attention to what I say—I can see it by your look; anyhow you've been warned. Well, go on! Do as you please; tomorrow morning you will tell me all about it."

He got up and went away, leaving me unable to make out whether he had meant to check my curiosity or whether he had not been amusing himself on the contrary by prodding it.

Until evening came my mind, in a state of confusion I cannot attempt to describe, was solely occupied by waiting for the moments to pass. Was I really in love with Isabelle? Doubtless not; but how could I have failed to think so when, stirred to the very heart by the violence of my excitement, I recognized in my curiosity all the symptoms of love —its quivering ardor, its impetuosity, its impatience? The Abbé's last words had only made me keener. What harm could Gratien do me? I was prepared to go through fire and water!

There was certainly something unusual brewing. That evening no one suggested a game. Directly after supper Mme de Saint-Auréol began to complain of her "gasteritis," as she called it, and retired without further excuse, while Mlle Verdure prepared her a hot drink. A few minutes later Mme Floche sent Casimir to bed and, as soon as he was gone, said:

"I believe Monsieur Lacase would very much like to follow suit; he looks dead with sleep."

And as I did not at once act on the hint, she added:

"I don't think any of us are inclined to sit up late."

Mlle Verdure got up to light the candles; the Abbé and I followed her; I saw Mme Floche bend over her husband, who was dozing in the *berline* by the fire; he rose at once and, taking the Baron by the arm, dragged him off unresisting and as if he understood what was wanted of him. On the landing, where everyone, candlestick in hand, went off each in his own direction, the Abbé wished me goodnight:

"Sleep well," said he with a meaning smile.

I shut the door of my room and then I waited. It was only nine o'clock. I heard Mme Floche come up and then Mlle Verdure. There was the continuation of a rather lively quarrel on the landing between Mme Floche and Mme de Saint-Auréol, who had come out of her room again, but they were too far off for me to catch any words. Then a sound of doors slamming; then nothing more.

I stretched myself on my bed the better to reflect. I thought of the Abbé's ironical hope that I should sleep well when he wished me good-night; I should have liked to know whether he himself was preparing for sleep or whether he would now indulge the curiosity he would not allow himself to show in my presence. But his room was in another part of the house, in the opposite wing to that in which I slept, and no plausible motive could justify my presence there. Yet which of us two, I wondered, if we were to meet in the passage, would look the greater fool? . . . Meditating thus, I was overtaken by an inexcusable, an absurd, an amazing circumstance—I fell asleep.

Yes, less excited, no doubt, than exhausted by my long hours of suspense, worn out too by my bad night the evening before, I fell into a deep sleep.

The sputtering of my dying candle woke me— or perhaps it was some faint vibration of the floor, which I had been vaguely conscious of during my sleep; certainly there had been steps in the passage. I sat up. At the same moment my candle went out; there I was in the dark, in a state of utter bewilderment. I had nothing to see by but a few matches; I struck one to look at my watch—it was almost half past eleven. I strained my ears—not a sound. I groped my way to the door and opened it.

No, my heart was not beating; I felt buoyant and alert in body; calm, wary, and determined in mind.

At the other end of the passage a glimmer of light streamed in on me from a large window; it did not shine steadily as in still nights, but flickered and at times died fitfully away, for the sky was overcast and the wind was driving heavy clouds across the moon. I had taken off my shoes and advanced noiselessly. . . . It was not too dark for me to find

my way to the observation post I had arranged for
myself in a little unused room next to Mme Floche's,
where I supposed the confabulation would take
place (it had at one time been occupied by M.
Floche, but he now preferred the neighborhood
of his books to that of his wife). The communicat-
ing door, which I had carefully bolted in order to
guard against surprises, had dropped a little, leaving a gap under the frame at the top, through which
I found it was possible to see; to reach this I had
to perch myself on the top of a chest of drawers
which I had pushed close up to the spot.

A ray of light now shone through this gap and,
reflected from the white ceiling, enabled me to see
my way. Everything was exactly as I had left it the
day before. I climbed onto the chest of drawers and
peered down into the next room. . . .

Isabelle de Saint-Auréol was there.

I saw her before me, only a few paces away. . . .
She was sitting on one of those low seats—ugly
things without backs, called, I believe, "poufs,"—
which it gave me something of a shock to see in this
ancient room, and which I did not remember noticing the day I took in the flowers. Mme Floche
was buried in a great tapestry-covered armchair;

on a little table at her side stood a lamp, which cast
a subdued light over them both. Isabelle had her
back to me; she was leaning forward, almost lying
across her old aunt's lap, so that at first I could
not see her face. Before long, however, she raised
her head. She had aged less than I expected, but I
could scarcely recognize the young girl of the miniature; her beauty certainly was not less, but it was
a beauty of a very different kind—more earthly,
grown more human, as it were. The angelic candor
of the portrait had given way to a passionate lan-
guor; the corners of her mouth, which the artist
had drawn half open, were now curled in an indefinable expression of discontent. A large traveling
cloak, a sort of waterproof, made, so it seemed, of
some rather cheap material, covered her dress
almost entirely, except where it was a little hitched
up and showed a skirt of shiny black silk, against
which her ungloved hand, holding a crumpled handkerchief, hung down, looking extraordinarily white
and fragile. On her head she wore a little befeathered
bonnet with silk strings, from under which a curl
of very black hair had escaped and fell over her
temple whenever she leaned forward. One might
have thought her in mourning but for a brilliant
beetle-green ribbon she wore round her neck.
Neither she nor Mme Floche were speaking; but

Isabelle, with her right hand, was gently stroking Mme Floche's arm and then she drew her hand toward her and covered it with kisses.

And now she was shaking her head, and her curls waved from left to right; at last she said, as though in repetition of some previous statement:

"Everything—I have really tried everything. I swear—"

"Don't swear, my poor child; I believe you without that," interrupted the poor old lady, putting her hand on Isabelle's head. They both spoke very low, as if afraid of being overheard.

Mme Floche raised herself, gently pushed away her niece, and, helping herself up by its arms, rose from her chair. Mlle de Saint-Auréol got up at the same time and followed her aunt for a few steps toward the writing-table from which Casimir had taken the miniature two days before. She stopped in front of a console table on which stood a great mirror and, while the old lady was fumbling in a drawer, caught sight in the glass of the emerald ribbon she was wearing round her neck; quickly unfastening it, she wound it round her finger, and before Mme Floche turned round, the bright ribbon had vanished and Isabelle had taken up a pensive attitude, her hands crossed on her knees, her eyes gazing into space. . . .

Mme Floche, poor old thing, was still holding her bunch of keys in one hand and in the. other the meager little bundle of notes she had taken out of the drawer; she was just going to seat herself again in her armchair when the door opposite that at which I was posted was suddenly flung open—and I could hardly restrain a cry of stupefaction. The Baronne was standing stiffly in the doorway, décolleté, rouged, in full ceremonial attire and her head surmounted by what looked like a gigantic feather brush of marabout. She was staggering under the weight of a great six-branched candelabra in which all the candles were burning, flooding her with their flickering light and shedding tears of wax all over the floor. She had come, no doubt, to the end of her strength, for she began by hastily making for the table and setting down the candelabra in front of the looking-glass; then, taking four skips back to her position in the doorway, she once more advanced, solemnly and with measured steps, stretching out at full length in front of her a hand loaded with enormous rings. In the middle of the room she stood still, turned stiffly toward her daughter, and, with hand still outstretched, shrieked in ear-splitting accents:

"Get thee behind me, ungrateful daughter! Your tears can no longer move me, and your protestations have forever lost the way to my heart."

The whole speech was delivered with no variation of tone at the topmost pitch of her voice. In the meantime Isabelle had thrown herself at her mother's feet and taken hold of her skirt; as she pulled it to one side, revealing two absurd little white satin slippers, she herself continued to strike her forehead on the floor, where a rug was spread over the boards. Mme de Saint-Auréol did not lower her eyes for an instant; still looking straight before her, with glances as piercing and icy as her voice, she continued:

"Is it not enough for you to have brought poverty into the dwelling of your parents? Are you contemplating a further—"

Here her voice suddenly failed her and she turned toward Mme Floche, who, making herself as small as she could, sat trembling in her armchair:

"And as for you, sister, if you are still so weak—" (then she repeated) "if you are still so unpardonably weak as to yield to her entreaties, even for one kiss—even for one mite—so true as I am your elder sister, I leave you, I recommend my household gods to Heaven, and I will never set eyes on you again."

I seemed to be looking on at a play. But since they were unconscious of being watched, for whose

benefit was it these two marionettes were acting
this tragedy? The attitudes and gestures of the
daughter seemed to me as exaggerated and as arti-
ficial as those of the mother. . . . The latter was
facing me, so that I saw Isabelle from behind, still
prostrate in the posture of a suppliant Esther; all
at once I caught sight of her feet: the shoes she
wore, as far as I could see through the coating of
mud that covered them, seemed to have tops of
puce-colored poult-de-soie; above them showed her
white stockings, across which the dripping, muddy
flounce of her lifted skirt had left a smear of dirt.
. . . And instantly the long story of adventure and
wretchedness told by these poor witnesses spoke
more loudly to my heart than all the old woman's
declamatory tirades. A sob rose in my throat; I
made up my mind to follow Isa through the garden when she left the house.

In the meantime Mme de Saint-Auréol had taken
three steps toward Mme Floche's chair.

"Come, give me those notes. Do you imagine I
don't see the paper you are crumpling in your hand?
Do you think me blind or mad? Give me the money,
I tell you!" And seizing the notes, she held them
melodramatically to the flame of one of the candles
in the candelabra. "I would rather burn them all"
(needless to say, she did nothing of the sort) "than

let her have a penny."

She slipped the notes into her pocket and resumed her theatrical attitude:

"Ungrateful daughter! Unnatural daughter! My bracelets and my necklaces, you know what road they took! Let my rings go the same way!"

So saying, with a dexterous movement of her outstretched hand, she let two or three drop on the floor. Like a famished dog after a bone, Isabelle flung herself upon them.

"Now go! We have nothing more to say to each other; I no longer acknowledge you."

Then, having taken an extinguisher from the bed-table, she extinguished one after the other all the candles in the candelabra and departed.

The room now seemed dark. Isabelle in the meantime had got up; she passed her fingers across her forehead, threw back her scattered curls, and adjusted her bonnet. With a swift shake she jerked up her cloak, which had slipped a little off her shoulders, and bent over Mme Floche to wish her good-by. The poor woman seemed trying to speak to her, but her voice was too weak for me to make out what she said. Isabelle silently pressed one of the old woman's trembling hands to her lips. An instant later, I darted in pursuit of her down the passage.

Just as I reached the stairs, I was arrested by the sound of voices and recognized one of them as Mlle Verdure's. Isabelle had already come upon her in the hall, and by leaning over the banisters, I could see them both. Olympe Verdure held a little lantern in her hand.

"Are you going away without giving him a kiss?" she said, and I understood they were talking of Casimir. "Don't you want to see him, then?"

"No, Loly; I'm too much in a hurry. Don't let him know I've been here."

There was silence—something was going on in dumbshow that I couldn't at first make out. The lantern was moving about and cast leaping shadows. Mlle Verdure advancing, Isabelle retreating, both of them had moved a few steps from their original positions; then I heard:

"Yes, yes; in remembrance of me. I've been keeping it such a long time. Now I'm old, what use would it be to me?"

"Loly! Loly! Of all I'm leaving here, there's no one so good as you."

Mlle Verdure put her arms round her. "Oh, poor darling! How wet she is!"

"Only my cloak—it's nothing. Let me go now."

"Take an umbrella, then."

"It's stopped raining."

"The lantern."

"No, I don't want it. The carriage is quite close. Good-by."

"Well then, good-by, my poor child. May God—" She ended with a sob. Mlle Verdure stayed for a few moments leaning out into the night, and a draft of damp air blew in from outside up the well of the staircase; then I heard her close the door and bolt it.

I could not get past Mlle Verdure. The key of the kitchen door was removed every night by Gratien. True, there was another door on the other side of the house by which I could easily have got out, but it was an immense way round; before I could have found her, Isabelle would have already got to her carriage. Ha! supposing I called her from my window. . . . I hurried back to my room. The moon was again obscured; I caught the sound of footsteps and waited a moment. A violent gust of wind arose and, as Gratien went in by the kitchen, I heard, through the whispering of the storm-tossed trees, the wheels of the carriage that bore away Isabelle de Saint-Auréol.

vii

I HAD DELAYED overlong, and as soon as I got back
to Paris I was beset by a thousand preoccupations
that turned my thoughts at length into other chan-
nels. The resolution I had made of returning to La
Quartfourche the following summer lessened my
regrets at not having been able to carry my adventure further. I was indeed beginning to forget
it when toward the end of January I received a
formal announcement of the deaths of M. and Mme
Floche. The two old people had resigned their gentle, tremulous souls into their Maker's hands within
a few days of one another. I recognized Mlle Verdure's handwriting on the envelope; but it was to
Casimir I wrote the banal expression of my regret
and sympathy. Two weeks later I received the following letter:

My dear Monsieur Gérard,

     [The child had always refused to call me by
my surname. "What is your name?" he had asked

me during one of our walks, the very day I had begun to talk familiarly with him.

["Why, you know it already, Casimir; I am
called Monsieur Lacase."

["No; not that name—the other?" he had
insisted.]

*It is is very kind of you to have written me
such a nice letter, and your letter was so nice because La Quartfourche is very sad now. My grandmother had a stroke on Thursday and couldn't
leave her room; then Mamma came back to La
Quartfourche and the Abbé went away because he
was made curé at Breuil. Then after that, my uncle and my aunt died. First my uncle died. He was
very fond of you. And then the Sunday after that
my aunt, who had been ill for three days. Mamma
had gone away. I was all alone with Loly and Delphine, Gratien's wife; she is very fond of me. And
it was very sad because my aunt didn't want to
leave me. But it couldn't be helped. And now I sleep
in the room next to Delphine's, because Loly had
to go to her brother-in-law's in the Orne. Gratien is
very kind to me too. He has shown me how to make
cuttings and grafts, which is very amusing, and I
am helping cut down the trees too.*

*You know the little paper what you wrote
your promise on. You must forget it because there's
no one here now for you to stay with. But I am very
sorry to think I shan't see you again because I was
very fond of you. But I haven't forgotten you.*

Your little friend,

Casimir

M. and Mme Floche's death had left me more or
less indifferent, but this awkward, artless letter
touched me. I was not free at the moment, but I determined to make an expedition of inquiry to La
Quartfourche as soon as the Easter holidays came
round. What did it matter to me that there was no
one for me to stay with? I could put up at Pont-
l'Évêque and hire a carriage from there. Need I
add that the thought of a possible meeting with the
mysterious Isabelle was as great an attraction as
my deep pity for the child? There were passages
in his letter that were incomprehensible; it was
difficult to link the facts together. . . . The old
lady's stroke, Isabelle's arrival, the Abbé's departure, the death of the old Floches, Isabelle's absence
at the time, the departure of Mlle Verdure—were
these a merely fortuitous series of events, or was
there some connection between them? Casimir could

not and the Abbé would not enlighten me. There was nothing for it but to wait till April. On the second day of my vacation I started.

At the Breuil station I caught sight of the Abbé just as he was getting into my train; I hailed him.

"So here you are back again," said he.

"Yes; as a matter of fact, I didn't think I should be returning so soon."

He got into my compartment. We were alone.

"Well! There have been changes since you left."

"Yes; I heard you had become curé at Breuil."

"Oh, I didn't mean that," and he made a gesture with his outspread hand which I remembered. "Did you get an announcement?"

"Yes; and I at once wrote a letter of condolence to your pupil. It was he who told me some of the news; but he wasn't very explicit. I very nearly wrote and asked you for details."

"You should have done so."

"I thought it wouldn't be very easy to get them out of you," I answered, laughing.

But the Abbé no doubt felt less necessity for discretion than when he was staying at La Quartfourche, and seemed inclined to talk.

"It's a wretched state of affairs, isn't it?" said he. "There's an end of the woods."

At first I did not understand; then a sentence of

Casimir's letter came back to my mind: "I am helping cut down the trees. . . ."

"What are they doing that for?" I asked ingenu-
ously.

"What for, my good sir? Go and ask the creditors.
But, after all, it's not their work; it's all being done
behind their backs. The place is mortgaged up to
the hilt. Mademoiselle de Saint-Auréol is making
off with as much as she can."

"Is she there?"

"As if you didn't know!"

"I merely guessed it from a few words that—"

"It's since she came back that everything has gone
to the dogs."

He caught himself up for a moment, but this time
the desire to speak was too much for him; he did not
even wait for me to question him and I thought it
wiser not to; he went on:

"How came she to hear of her mother's stroke?
I never made out. When she learned that the old
Baronne couldn't leave her chair, in she marched
with all her baggage, and Madame Floche hadn't
the heart to turn her out. It was after that that I
went away."

"It was very sad your leaving Casimir like
that."

"Possibly, but it was not my place to stay in the

same house with a shameless— But I forgot you stood up for her."

"I shall very likely continue to do so, Monsieur le Curé."

"Very good. Very good. Yes, I know; Mademoiselle Verdure stood up for her too. She stood up for her until the day the old folks died."

I was amused to notice that the Abbé had almost entirely dropped the elegant language he had favored while he was at La Quartfourche, and had adopted the speech and manners peculiar to the curés of Normandy villages. He went on with his train of thought:

"She thought it odd too when they died so soon one after the other."

"Did they—?"

"I say nothing," and he pursed up his lips in his old way, but immediately started off again:

"All the same, there was a good deal of gossip in the neighborhood. People weren't pleased to see the niece come into the property. And you see even Verdure thought it best to leave too."

"Who looks after Casimir?"

"Ah! Even you understand that his mother is not a proper person to be with the child. He spends nearly the whole of his time with the Chointreuils —you know, the gardener and his wife."

"Gratien?"

"Yes, Gratien; he tried to prevent the park trees from being cut down; but there was nothing he could do. It's simply ruin."

"But surely the Floches had money?"

"Oh, that all went the first day, my dear sir. Two of the three farms on the estate belonged to Madame Floche, but it's many a long day since they were bought up by the tenants. The third, the little farm of Les Fonds still belongs to the Baronne; there was no tenant and Gratien ran it; but it will be put up for sale with the rest."

"La Quartfourche is to be put up for sale?"

"At auction. But it can't be done before the end of the summer. In the meantime I'll beg you to believe that my fine lady is making what she can. It's true she will have to end by swallowing the pill— but by then half the trees will have gone."

"But how can she find anyone to buy, if she hasn't the right to sell?"

"Oh, you're very innocent still! When things are going for nothing, there's always someone to buy."

"Any deputy sheriff might prevent it."

"The deputy sheriff is in collusion with the creditors' agent, who has settled down there"; he stopped and whispered in my ear: "he sleeps with her, since you want to know everything."

"Monsieur Floche's books and papers?" I asked, without appearing disturbed by his last remark.

"There is shortly to be a sale of the library and furniture—or, to be more accurate, an execution. Fortunately no one there suspects the value of some of the books, or they would have disappeared long ago."

"But suppose some rascal turned up—"

"No fear; the seals have been affixed; they won't be removed till the inventory has to be made."

"And what does the Baronne say to it all?"

"She has no idea what is going on; her food is taken to her in her room; she doesn't even know her daughter is there."

"You haven't mentioned the Baron."

"He died three weeks ago in a nursing home at Caen just after we had managed to get him into it."

We had reached Pont-l'Évêque. A priest came to meet Abbé Santal, who took leave of me after having told me of a hotel and a livery stable.

The carriage I hired next day dropped me at the entrance to the park; it was settled the man should come and pick me up in a couple of hours, after the horses had rested in a neighboring farm stable.

I found the iron gates wide open; the road had been plowed up by heavy carts. I was expecting the most frightful devastation, and it gave me a joyful surprise as I entered to find my old friend the "peach-leaved beech" in full bud; I did not stop to reflect that it no doubt owed its life only to the inferior quality of its wood; as I went on my way, I saw that the finest trees had already fallen to the ax. Before advancing farther into the park, I wanted to revisit the little lodge where I had discovered Isabelle's letter; but the broken lock was now replaced by a padlock on the door (I learned afterward that the woodcutters used the lodge to keep their tools and coats in). I turned my steps toward the château. The path I followed was straight, bordered on each side by low bushes; it did not come out at the front of the house but at the side offices and led to the kitchen, almost opposite which was a small gate opening into the kitchen garden; I was still some way from it when I saw Gratien come out of the garden with a basket of vegetables; he saw me without at first recognizing me; I hailed him and he came up to me.

"Well, I never! Monsieur Lacase!" he exclaimed. "We weren't expecting *you* at this time of day!" He stood looking at me, wagging his head and not attempting to hide his vexation at my appearance;

he added, however, more mildly: "The boy will be pleased to see you, though."

We had taken a few steps in the direction of the kitchen without speaking; he signed to me to wait for him while he went in to put down his basket.

"So you've come to see what's going on at La Quartfourche," said he, more civilly, as he came back.

"And it seems things are not going very well?"

I looked at him; his chin was trembling; he stood without answering; then, abruptly seizing me by the arm, he dragged me up to the lawn in front of the house. There lay the dead body of a monster oak, underneath which I remembered having taken shelter in the autumn. It had been stripped of its branches before being felled and now they were piled all around it in heaps of logs and bundles of faggots.

"Do you know how much a tree like that is worth?" said he. "Twelve pistoles! And do you know what they've paid for it? For that, and the others too—five francs!"

I did not know that in that part of the world a ten-franc piece was called a pistole; but it was not the moment for explanations. Gratien went on with a choking voice. I turned to look at his face; he was wiping away tears or sweat with the back of his hand.

"Oh, the ruffians!" he exclaimed, clenching his fists, "the ruffians! When I hear their hatchets and their axes I'm like to go mad, sir; the blows fall on my own head; I want to call out 'Help! Murder!' I want to use a hatchet on them myself. I want to kill them! I spent half the day yesterday in the cellar; the noise wasn't so loud there. At first it amused the boy to watch the woodcutters at their work; when the tree was ready to fall, they called him to pull the rope; but when the ruffians brought their felling nearer the house, he didn't think it so funny. 'Oh, not that one!' he said, 'not this one!' 'My poor lad,' says I, 'don't worry about this or that—they won't leave you a single one.' I've told him straight he won't be able to stay on at La Quartfourche; but he's too young yet; he can't get it into his head that none of it's his any longer. If only we could be kept on at the little farm; I'd have him to live with us gladly, for sure; but it'll be bought by the Lord knows who, and what sort of rascal they'll put in instead of us? . . . Look, sir, I'm not so very old yet, but I'd liefer have died than see all that."

"Who is living in the château now?"

"I don't want to know. The boy, he eats with us in the kitchen; it's better so. Madame la Baronne can't leave her room. Lucky for her, poor lady! . . . Delphine takes her her meals, by the back stairs, so as not to come across certain people we won't mention. They have someone else to wait on them, but we don't speak."

"Isn't there going to be a sale of the furniture soon?"

"When that comes we'll try and get Madame la Baronne to the farm—until that's put up for sale too with the château."

"And Made—and her daughter?" I asked hesitatingly, for I was at a loss what to call her.

"I don't care where she goes, as long as it isn't near us. To think that all this has happened because of her."

I understood then—anger so deep and so grave trembled in his voice—that this man might have been capable of committing a crime in defense of his masters' honor.

"Is she in the house now?"

"It's likely she's walking in the park at this hour. She doesn't seem to feel it; she watches the woodcutters at work; some days she even talks to them, shamelessly. But when it rains she doesn't leave her room—see, up there, the corner one. She stands

close to the window and looks out at the garden. If
her man wasn't at Lisieux just now, I shouldn't be
about as I am. Ah, Monsieur Lacase, they're fine
gentry, for sure! If my poor old masters came back
and saw what's going on in their home, they'd soon
want to go back to the place they came from!"

"Is Casimir anywhere about?"

"I think he's in the park too. Shall I go and call
him for you?"

"No; I shall easily find him. Good-by for the
present. I shall see Delphine and you again no doubt
before I leave."

The havoc caused by the woodcutters seemed
still more cruel at this time of year when everything was awakening to new life. Young shoots were
already swelling in the milder air; buds were bursting and every severed branch was weeping tears of
sap. I walked on slowly, the stricken landscape moving me not so much to sadness as to intenser consciousness; and perhaps the smell of vegetation
that exhaled so powerfully from dying tree and
travailing earth went a little to my head like wine.
I was hardly sensible of the contrast between the
corpses that strewed the ground and the reawaken-
ing spring; the park lay more open thus to the light
that bathed both death and life alike in a golden
glory; but yet the tragic song of the blows that

rang through the distance, filling the air with a
funereal solemnity, kept secret time to the happy
beatings of my heart; and the old love-letter I had
brought with me, though I had sworn to myself not
to use it, burned my breast as from time to time
I pressed it to my heart. "Nothing shall stand in my
way today," I said to myself, and I smiled to feel
my step grow quicker at the mere thought of Isabelle; my will was in abeyance; it was a hidden
power within that drove me. How strange it was
that, by some overabundance of life in me, the note
of savage violence that all this devastation added to
the beauty of the landscape only intensified my
pleasure in it; how strange that the Abbé's calum-
nies had so little succeeded in detaching me from
Isabelle, and that all I heard about her only gave a
secret relish to the keenness of my desire! . . .
What was it that kept her in this spot which was
so peopled with hideous memories? The sale of La
Quartfourche could bring her—would leave her—
nothing. Why had she not fled from it? And I
dreamed of bearing her off that very evening in
my carriage; I walked more hurriedly, I was almost
running, indeed, when suddenly, there in the distance before me, I caught sight of her. There was
no doubt about it. It was she, in mourning and
bareheaded, sitting on the trunk of a felled tree

that had fallen across the path. My heart was beating so fast that I had to stop for a moment or two; then I went up to her slowly—a calm, indifferent gentleman taking a stroll.

"Excuse me, madame—can you tell me whether this is La Quartfourche?"

Beside her on the tree-trunk was a little work-basket full of spools, sewing-materials, and pieces of crape, some rolled up in bundles, others lying loose; she was employed in arranging one or two of these scraps on a dowdy little felt hat that she was holding in her hand; a green ribbon she had no doubt just torn from it was lying on the ground. She was wearing a very short black cloth cape over her shoulders, and when she raised her head, I noticed the common little clasp at the neck. She had no doubt seen me in the distance, for she did not seem surprised by my voice.

"Have you come about buying the place?" she said, and my heart beat as I recognized her voice. How beautiful I thought her uncovered brow!

"Oh, simply to look at it. The park gates were open and I saw there were people about inside. But perhaps it was indiscreet of me to come in?"

"Anybody who likes may come in now!" She heaved a deep sigh but returned again to her work as if we could have nothing more to say to each other.

I did not know how to continue the conversation; it was an opportunity that would probably never offer itself again, that would certainly be decisive; and yet I did not feel that the moment had come to precipitate matters; in my anxiety to be cautious, therefore, my heart and head filled with hopes and questions I did not as yet dare formulate, I remained speechless, poking with the end of my stick at some little chips of wood on the ground, so embarrassed, so awkward, and so impertinent withal, that at last she raised her eyes, stared at me, and was, I thought, going to burst out laughing; but—no doubt because in those days I wore a soft hat and my hair long and did not seem to have any very urgent occupation—all she said was:

"Are you an artist?"

"Unfortunately not," I answered, smiling; "but that doesn't prevent me from appreciating poetry." And though I did not as yet dare to look at her, I felt her eyes resting on me. Our hypocritical commonplaces were odious and I hate having to repeat them.

"How beautiful the park is!" I went on.

She seemed to wish for nothing better than to

talk and was only embarrassed, like myself. by the difficulty of knowing how to start the conversation, for she exclaimed at once that unfortunately at this time of year the park was still shivering with cold and barely awakened out of its winter sleep, and that it was impossible to judge of what it was like in autumn—"at least of what it used to be like," she corrected herself; "for what will be left of it when the woodcutters have finished their dreadful work? . . ."

"Couldn't they be prevented?" I cried.

"Prevented!" she repeated ironically, and shrugged her shoulders; and I thought she was showing me her shabby felt hat to bear witness to her destitution, but she merely picked it up in order to put it on (she wore it tipped back so as to leave her forehead bare); then she began to arrange her pieces of crape as if she were getting ready to go. I stooped down, picked up the green ribbon at her feet, and handed it to her.

"What is the use of it now?" she said without taking it. "You see I am in mourning."

I immediately said how sorry I had been to hear of M. and Mme Floche's death and recently too of the Baron's; and as she expressed astonishment at my having known her family, I told her I had spent ten days with them last October.

"Then why did you pretend not to know where you were just now?" she rejoined abruptly.

"I had to find an excuse for speaking to you."

Then, without as yet showing my hand too openly, I began to tell her of the passionate curiosity that had kept me at La Quartfourche day after day in hopes of meeting her and (I did not mention the night on which I had watched her so indiscreetly) of my regret at having to go back to Paris without having seen her.

"What gave you such a desire to know me?"

She no longer made as though to go. I had dragged up a big bundle of wood on which I sat down close to her and facing her; I was lower than she and had to look up in order to see her face; she was childishly busied in rolling up her crape ribbons into little balls and I could not catch her eyes. I spoke of her miniature and of my anxiety to know what had become of the picture I had fallen in love with; but she could not tell me.

"I suppose it will be found when the seals are removed—and it will be put up at auction with the rest," she added with a hard laugh that was painful to hear. "You will be able to get it for a few sous if you still have a fancy for it."

I protested I was grieved to see she did not take me seriously; that it was only their expression that was sudden, but that these feelings had occupied me for a long time past; she remained impassive, however, resolved, apparently, to have nothing more to do with me. Time was pressing. But had I not in my possession something that would force her defenses? The ardent letter lay quivering in my hand. I had prepared some story or other of an old connection between my family and the Gonfrevilles, thinking it might induce her to speak; but at that moment I felt the absurdity of such a falsehood and began quite simply to relate by what mysterious chance the letter—I held it out to her—had fallen into my hands.

"Ah! I implore you," I cried, "do not tear it up! Give it back to me. . . ."

She had turned deadly pale and kept the letter open on her knees for a few moments without reading it; with vaguely staring eyes and fluttering eyelids, she murmured:

"Forgotten it! How could I have forgotten it?"

"You must have thought it had reached him, that he had come for it. . . ."

She was not listening to me. I made a motion to take the letter back again, but she misunderstood it.

"Leave me," she cried, pushing my hand away roughly. She rose and tried to go. On my knees before her, I held her back.

"Don't be afraid of me," I cried; "can't you see I wish you no harm?" And as she sat down again, or rather sank down powerless, I begged her not to be angry with me if chance had chosen me to be her involuntary confidant, and implored her to complete a confidence that I swore not to betray; oh, would she not speak to me now as to a true friend who knew nothing but what she herself had told me?

The tears I shed as I spoke were more convincing perhaps than my words.

"Alas!" I went on, "I know what a melancholy fate deprived you of your lover that very evening. . . . But how did you learn your loss? What did you think that night as you were waiting for him, prepared to fly? What did you do when you saw he was not coming?"

"Since you know everything," said she in a heart-broken voice, "you must know that there was no question of my expecting him, once I had forewarned Gratien."

The dreadful truth came upon me with such a flash of intuition that the next words broke from me like a cry:

"What! It was *you* who had him killed?"

Dropping the letter, the workbasket, and all its contents on to the ground, she buried her face in her hands and began to sob desperately. I leaned toward her and tried to take one of her hands in mine.

"No! You are ungrateful—brutal!"

My rash exclamation had cut short her confidences and hardened her heart against me; I still remained, however, sitting in front of her, firmly resolved not to leave her till she had explained herself more fully. Her sobs at last subsided; I persuaded her gently that now she had said so much, she could not possibly keep silent as to the rest, but that a sincere confession would not make me think ill of her, and nothing she could say would grieve me more than a refusal to speak. With her elbows on her knees, and her clasped hands hiding her face, this is what she told me:

She had written the letter in a state of passionate excitement during the watches of the night preceding the one she had fixed on for her flight; the next morning she had taken it to the lodge and slipped it into the hiding-place that Blaise de Gonfreville knew of and from which she counted on his shortly taking it. But as soon as she got back to the château, as soon as she found herself again in the room she had wished to leave forever, she had been overcome by a dreadful, unspeakable misgiving—fear of the unknown liberty she had so savagely desired, fear of the lover she still longed for, of herself, and of what she dared not venture. Yes, she had made the resolve; yes, she had repressed her scruples, swallowed her shame, but now that nothing held her back, now that the door stood open for her flight, her heart suddenly failed her. The idea of flight became odious to her—intolerable; she rushed to tell Gratien that the Vicomte de Gonfreville had planned to carry her off that very night, that he would be found toward evening loitering in the neighborhood of the lodge gates, and that he must be prevented from coming farther.

I expressed astonishment that she had not simply gone herself to get back her letter and replace it by another in which she might have dissuaded her lover from the mad scheme. But she evaded all the questions I put to her and kept repeating with tears that she knew I should not be able to understand her, that she could not explain herself better, but that at the time she had felt as little able to repulse her lover as to follow him, that fear had paralyzed her to such an extent that she was physically incapable of returning to the lodge; that besides, at that time of day, the parents she dreaded so were watching her, which was really the reason she had been obliged to have recourse to Gratien.

"Could I imagine he would take my wild words so seriously? I thought he would merely keep him off. . . . An hour later I was startled by hearing

a gunshot in the direction of the gates; but my
thoughts recoiled from such a horrible supposition
and I refused to contemplate it; on the contrary,
since I had spoken to Gratien, I felt almost joyful,
with a load taken off my heart and mind. . . . But
when night came, when the hour that should have
been that of my flight drew near—ah, in spite of
myself, I began to feel expectant, I began to feel
hopeful once more; a kind of confidence, which yet
I knew was unfounded, mingled with my despair;
I could not realize that the cowardice, the weakness
of a moment had shattered my long dream at one
blow; I was still not awake; yes, it was still in a
dream that I went down into the garden, ears and
eyes on the watch for every noise, every shadow;
I waited—I waited on and on. . . ."

She began to sob again.

"No, I was not waiting for anything any more,"
she went on; "I tried to deceive myself and out of
pity for my own self I acted the part of someone
waiting and expecting. I had sat down by the lawn,
on the lowest step of the perron; my heart too dry
to shed a tear; thinking of nothing, knowing neither
who I was, nor where I was, nor what I had come
there to do. The moon, which had been shining on
the grass, disappeared; then an icy shudder seized
me; I wished it could have frozen me to death.

Next day I fell seriously ill and the doctor who was called in informed my mother of my pregnancy."

She stopped for a few moments.

"You know now what you wanted to know. If I were to go on with my story, it would be that of another woman, and you would not recognize the Isabelle of the locket."

As it was, I could hardly recognize the Isabelle my imagination had fallen in love with. Her tale, it is true, was interlarded with interjections; she recriminated against fate; she lamented that in this world poetry and sentiment are always in the wrong; but it grieved me not to hear in her melodious voice any of the warm harmonics of the heart. Not a word of regret for anyone but herself! "What!" I thought, "is *that* the only way she can love? . . ."

I began to pick up the small objects that had fallen out of her overturned workbasket. I had no further desire to question her; I suddenly lost all curiosity as to her person and her life and stood before her like a child with a toy he has broken in order to discover its mystery; and even the physical attraction that was still hers no longer stirred in me the slightest trouble of the senses—nor even the voluptuous droop of her eyelids, which a moment before had made me tremble. We spoke of her want of means; and as I asked her what she intended to do:

"I shall try to give lessons," she replied; "piano or singing lessons. I have a very good technique."

"Ah! You sing?"

"Yes, and play the piano. I once worked very hard at it. I was a pupil of Thalberg's. . . . I am very fond of poetry too." And as I found nothing to say: "I am sure you know some by heart! Won't you repeat me something?"

Distaste, disgust for this trivial talk about poetry, finally drove love from my heart. I rose to take my leave.

"Oh, are you going already?"

"I am sorry, but you must see yourself that it is better for me to leave you now. Try to imagine that last autumn, when I was staying with your people, the drowsy air of La Quartfourche lulled me to sleep, that I fell in love with a dream, and that I have just waked up. Good-by."

A little limping form appeared at the farther end of the path.

"There is Casimir, I think. He will be glad to see me."

"He is coming here. Wait for him."

The boy came along in little hops; he was carrying a rake on his shoulder.

"If you will allow me, I will go to meet him. It might make him feel shy to see me with you. Excuse me." And hurrying over my farewells as awkwardly as I well could, I bowed respectfully and left her.

I never saw Isabelle de Saint-Auréol again and heard nothing more of her. Yes, once though. When I returned to La Quartfourche the following autumn, Gratien told me that just before the sale of the furniture she had been deserted by the estate agent and had gone off with a coachman.

"You see, Monsieur Lacase," he added sagaciously, "she never could live alone; she always had to have a man of some sort."

The La Quartfourche library was sold in the middle of the summer. In spite of my instructions, I was given no notice; and I think the Caen bookseller who was in charge of the sale was far from anxious to have me or any other serious connoisseur present. I learned later on with amazement and indignation that the famous Bible had been sold for seventy francs to a secondhand bookseller in the neighborhood, and resold immediately afterward for three hundred francs—I could never find out to whom. As for the seventeenth-century manuscripts,

they were not even mentioned in the catalogue and
were knocked down as waste paper.

I should have liked at any rate to have been
present at the sale of the furniture, for I had intended to buy a few small objects in memory of the
Floches; but I was notified too late and arrived at
Pont-l'Évêque only in time to be present at the sale
of the house property and farms. La Quartfourche
was knocked down for a trifling sum to the estate
agent Moser-Schmidt, who was on the point of turning the park into grassland, when an American
client bought it; I don't exactly know why, for he
never returned to the country and leaves the park
and château in the condition you saw.

As in those days I was far from well off, I meant
to attend the sale merely as a spectator, but I had
been to see Casimir that morning, and as I listened
to the bidding, I was filled with such compunction
at the thought of the poor little fellow's plight that
I suddenly resolved to settle him on the farm that
Gratien had told me he wanted to occupy. You didn't
know that it was my property? I ran up the bidding
almost before I was aware of it; it was folly; but
the poor child's melancholy pleasure more than
recompensed me.

I spent the Easter holidays and the following
summer vacation in the little farmhouse with

Gratien and Casimir. Old Mme de Saint-Auréol was still living; we had managed somehow or other to give her the best room; she was now in her dotage, but able to recognize me and remember my name more or less:

"How kind of you, Monsieur de Las Cases! How kind of you!" she kept repeating when she first saw me again. For she flattered herself that I had come back solely to visit her.

"They are making alterations up at the château. It will be very fine!" she said to me confidentially, by way of explaining to me—or to herself—her change of circumstances.

The day the furniture was put up for sale, she had been rolled out of the drawing-room on to the perron steps in her big armchair; the deputy sheriff had been introduced as a celebrated architect who had come from Paris on purpose to supervise the building alterations (she easily believed everything that flattered her); then Gratien, Casimir, and Delphine had carried her to the room in the farm-house which she had never left again, though she lingered on for another three years.

It was during those first summer holidays, which I spent on my farm, that I made the acquaintance of the B.'s, whose eldest daughter I afterward married. La R., which came to us after the death of my parents-in-law, is not, as you saw, very far from La Quartfourche; two or three times a year I go over and have a talk with Gratien and Casimir. They cultivate their farm very well and pay their small rent regularly. That was where I went this afternoon when I left you.

The night was far advanced by the time Gérard had finished telling us his story. But it was nevertheless that same night that Jammes wrote his fourth elegy before going to sleep—the one that begins:

"You asked me to write an elegy on the deserted park where the great gales . . ."

THE
PASTORAL SYMPHONY

FIRST NOTEBOOK

10 February 189—

THE SNOW HAS been falling continuously for the last three days and all the roads are blocked. It has been impossible for me to go to R——, where I have been in the habit of holding a service twice a month for the last fifteen years. This morning not more than thirty of my flock were gathered together in La Brévine chapel.

I will take advantage of the leisure this enforced confinement affords me to think over the past and to set down how I came to take charge of Gertrude.

I propose to write here the whole history of her formation and development, for I seem to have called up out of the night her sweet and pious soul for no other end but adoration and love. Blessed be the Lord for having entrusted me with this task!

Two years and six months ago I had just driven back one afternoon from La Chaux-de-Fonds when a little girl who was a stranger to me came up in a

great hurry to take me to a place about five miles
away where she said an old woman lay dying. My
horse was still in the shafts, so I made the child get
into the carriage and set off at once, after first pro-
viding myself with a lantern, as I thought it likely I
should not be able to get back before dark.

I had supposed myself to be perfectly acquainted
with the whole countryside in the neighborhood of
my parish; but when we had passed La Saudraie
farm, the child made me take a road that I had never
ventured down before. About two miles farther on,
however, I recognized on the left-hand side a mysterious little lake where I had sometimes been to
skate as a young man. I had not seen it for fifteen
years, for none of my pastoral duties take me that
way; I could not have said where it lay and it had so
entirely dropped out of my mind that when I suddenly recognized it in the golden enchantment of
the rose-flecked evening sky, I felt as though I had
seen it before only in a dream.

The road ran alongside the stream that falls out
of the lake, cut across the extreme end of the forest,
and then skirted a peat-bog. I had certainly never
been there before.

The sun was setting and for a long time we had
been driving in the shade when my young guide
pointed out a cottage on the hillside which would

have seemed uninhabited but for a tiny thread of smoke that rose from the chimney, looking blue in the shade and brightening as it reached the gold of the sky. I tied the horse up to an apple tree close by and then followed the child into the dark room where the old woman had just died.

The gravity of the landscape, the silence and solemnity of the hour had struck me to the heart. A woman still in her youth was kneeling beside the bed. The child, whom I had taken to be the deceased woman's granddaughter, but who was only her servant, lighted a smoky tallow dip and then stood motionless at the foot of the bed. During our long drive I had tried to get her to talk, but had not succeeded in extracting two words from her.

The kneeling woman rose. She was not a relation as I had first supposed, but only a neighbor, a friend, whom the servant girl had brought there when she saw her mistress's strength failing, and who now offered to watch by the dead body. The old woman, she said, had passed away painlessly. We agreed together on the arrangements for the burial and the funeral service. As often before in this out-of-the-world country, it fell to me to settle everything. I was a little uneasy, I admit, at leaving the house, in spite of the poverty of its appearance, in the sole charge of this neighbor and of the little servant girl.

But it seemed very unlikely that there was any treasure hidden away in a corner of this wretched dwelling . . . and what else could I do? I inquired nevertheless whether the old woman had left any heirs.

Upon this, the woman took the candle and held it up so as to light the corner of the hearth, and I could make out crouching in the fireplace, and apparently asleep, a nondescript-looking creature, whose face was almost entirely hidden by a thick mass of hair.

"The blind girl there—she's a niece, the servant says. That's all that's left of the family, it seems. She must be sent to the poorhouse; I don't see what else can be done with her."

I was shocked to hear the poor thing's future disposed of in this way in her presence and afraid such rough words might give her pain.

"Don't wake her up," I said softly, as a hint to the woman that she should at any rate lower her voice.

"Oh, I don't think she's asleep. But she's an idiot; she can't speak or understand anything, I'm told. I have been in the room since this morning and she has hardly so much as stirred. I thought at first she was deaf; the servant thinks not, but that the old woman was deaf herself and never uttered a word to her, nor to anyone else; she hadn't opened her mouth for a long time past except to eat and drink."

"How old is she?"

"About fifteen, I suppose. But as to that, I know no more about it than you do. . . ."

It did not immediately occur to me to take charge of the poor, forlorn creature myself; but after I had prayed—or, to be more accurate, while I was still praying on my knees between the woman and the little servant girl, who were both kneeling too—it suddenly came upon me that God had set a kind of obligation in my path and that I could not shirk it without cowardice. When I rose, I had decided to take the girl away that very evening, though I had not actually asked myself what I should do with her afterward, nor into whose charge I should put her. I stayed a few moments longer gazing at the old woman's sleeping face, with its puckered mouth, looking like a miser's purse with strings tightly drawn so as to let nothing escape. Then, turning toward the blind girl, I told the neighbor of my intention.

"Yes, it is better she should not be there tomorrow when they come to take the body away," said she. And that was all.

Many things would be easily accomplished but for the imaginary objections men sometimes take a pleasure in inventing. From our childhood upwards, how often have we been prevented from doing one thing or another we should have liked to do, simply by hearing people about us repeat: "He won't be able to . . ."!

The blind girl allowed herself to be taken away like a lifeless block. The features of her face were regular, rather fine, but utterly expressionless. I took a blanket off the mattress where she must have usually slept, in a corner under a staircase that led from the room to the loft.

The neighbor was obliging and helped me wrap her up carefully, for the night was very clear and chilly; after having lighted the carriage lamp, I started home, taking the girl with me. She sat huddled up against me—a soulless lump of flesh, with no sign of life beyond the communication of an obscure warmth. The whole way home I was thinking: "Is she asleep? And what can this black sleep be like? . . . And in what way do her waking hours differ from her sleeping? But this darkened body is surely tenanted; an immured soul is waiting there for a ray of Thy grace, O Lord, to touch it. Wilt Thou perhaps allow my love to dispel this dreadful darkness? . . ."

I have too much regard for the truth to pass over in silence the unpleasant welcome I had to encounter on my return home. My wife is a garden of virtues; and in the times of trouble we have sometimes gone through I have never for an instant had cause to doubt the stuff of which her heart is made; but it does not do to take her natural charity by surprise. She is an orderly person, careful neither to go beyond nor to fall short of her duty. Even her charity is measured, as though love were not an inexhaustible treasure. This is the only point on which we differ. . . .

Her first thoughts when she saw me bring home the girl that evening broke from her in this exclamation:

"What kind of job have you saddled yourself with now?"

As always happens when we have to come to an understanding, I began by telling the children—who were standing round, open-mouthed and full of curiosity and surprise—to leave the room. Ah, how different this welcome was from what I could have wished! Only my dear little Charlotte began to dance and clap her hands when she understood that something new, something alive, was coming out of the carriage. But the others, who have been well trained by their mother, very soon damped the child's pleasure and made her fall into step.

There was a moment of great confusion. And as neither my wife nor the children yet knew that they had to do with a blind person, they could not understand the extreme care with which I guided her footsteps. I myself was disconcerted by the odd moans the poor afflicted creature began to utter as soon as I let go her hand, which I had held in mine during the whole drive. There was nothing human in the sounds she made; they were more like the plaintive whines of a puppy. Torn away for the first time as she had been from the narrow round of customary sensations that had formed her universe, her knees now failed her; but when I pushed forward a chair, she sank on the floor in a heap, as if she were incapable of sitting down; I then led her up to the fireplace and she regained her calm a little as soon as she was able to crouch down in the same position in which I had first seen her beside the old woman's fire, leaning against the chimney-piece. In the carriage too, she had slipped off the seat and spent the whole drive huddled up at my feet. My wife, however, whose instinctive impulses are always the best, came to my help; it is her reflection that is constantly at odds with her heart and very often gets the better of it.

"What do you mean to do with *that*?" she asked when the girl had settled down.

I shivered in my soul at this use of the word *that*, and had some difficulty in restraining a movement of indignation. As I was still under the spell of my long and peaceful meditation, however, I controlled myself. Turning toward the whole party, who were standing round in a circle again, I placed my hand on the blind girl's head and said as solemnly as I could:

"I have brought back the lost sheep."

But Amélie will not admit that there can be anything unreasonable or superreasonable in the teaching of the Gospel. I saw she was going to object, and it was then I made a sign to Jacques and Sarah, who, as they are accustomed to our little conjugal differences and have not much natural curiosity (not enough, I often think), led the two younger children out of the room.

Then, as my wife still remained silent and a little irritated, I thought, by the intruder's presence: "You needn't mind speaking before her," I said. "The poor child doesn't understand."

Upon this Amélie began to protest that she had absolutely nothing to say—which is her usual prelude to the lengthiest explanations—and there was nothing for her to do but to submit, as usual, to all my most unpractical vagaries, however contrary to custom and good sense they might be. I have already said that I had not in the least made up my mind what I was going to do with the child. It had not occurred to me, or only in the vaguest way, that there was any possibility of taking her into our house permanently, and I may almost say it was Amélie herself who first suggested it to me by asking whether I didn't think there were "enough of us in the house already"? Then she declared that I always hurried on ahead without taking any thought for those who could not keep up with me, that for her part she considered five children quite enough, and that since the birth of Claude (who at that very moment set up a howl from his cradle, as if he had heard his name) she had as much as she could put up with and that she couldn't stand any more.

At the beginning of her outburst some of Christ's words rose from my heart to my lips; I kept them back, however, for I never think it becoming to allege the authority of the Holy Book as an excuse for my conduct. But when she spoke of her fatigue, I was struck with confusion, for I must admit it has more than once happened to me to let my wife suffer from the consequences of my impulsive and inconsiderate zeal. In the meantime, however, her recriminations had enlightened me as to my duty; I begged Amélie therefore, as mildly as possible, to consider whether she would not have done the same in my place and whether she could have possibly abandoned a creature who had been so obviously left without anyone to help her; I added that I was under no illusion as to the extra fatigue the charge of this new inmate would add to the cares of the household, and that I regretted I was not more often able to help her with them. In this way I pacified her as best I could, begging her at the same time not to visit her anger on the innocent girl, who had done nothing to deserve it. Then I pointed out that Sarah was now old enough to be more of a help to her and that Jacques was no longer in need of her care. In short, God put into my mouth the right words to help her accept what I am sure she would have undertaken of her own accord if the circumstances had given her time to reflect and if I had not forestalled her decision without consulting her.

I thought the cause was almost gained, and my dear Amélie was already approaching Gertrude with the kindest intentions; but her irritation suddenly blazed up again higher than ever when, on taking up the lamp to look at the child more closely, she discovered her to be in a state of unspeakable dirt.

"Why, she's filthy!" she cried. "Go and brush yourself quickly. No, not here. Go and shake your clothes outside. Oh dear! Oh dear! The children will be covered with them. There's nothing in the world I hate so much as vermin."

It cannot be denied that the poor child was crawling with them; and I could not prevent a feeling of disgust as I thought how close I had kept her to me during our long drive.

When I came back a few minutes later, having cleaned myself as best I could, I found my wife had sunk into an armchair and with her head in her hands was giving way to a fit of sobbing.

"I did not mean to put your fortitude to such a test," I said tenderly. "In any case it is late tonight and too dark to do anything. I will sit up and keep the fire going and the child can sleep beside it. Tomorrow we will cut her hair and wash her properly. You need not attend to her until you have got over your repugnance." And I begged her not to say anything of that to the children.

It was supper time. My protégée, at whom our old Rosalie cast many a scowling glance as she waited on us, greedily devoured the plateful of soup I handed her. The meal was a silent one. I should have liked to relate my adventure, to talk to the children and touch their hearts by making them understand and feel the strangeness of such a condition of total deprivation. I should have liked to rouse their pity, their sympathy for the guest God had sent us; but I was afraid of reviving Amélie's irritation. It seemed as though the word had been passed to take no notice of what had happened and to forget all about it, though certainly not one of us can have been thinking of anything else.

I was extremely touched when, more than an hour after everyone had gone to bed and Amélie had left me, I saw my little Charlotte steal gently through the half-open door in her nightdress and bare feet; she flung her arms round my neck and hugged me fiercely.

"I didn't say good-night to you properly," she murmured.

Then, pointing with her little forefinger to the blind girl, who was now peacefully slumbering and whom she had been curious to see again before going to sleep:

"Why didn't I kiss her too?" she whispered.

"You shall kiss her tomorrow. We must let her be now. She is asleep," I said as I went with her to the door.

Then I sat down again and worked till morning, reading or preparing my next sermon.

"Certainly," I remember thinking, "Charlotte seems much more affectionate than the elder children, but when they were her age, I believe they all got round me too. My big boy Jacques, nowadays so distant and reserved . . . One thinks them tender-hearted, when really they are only coaxing and wheedling one."

27 February

The snow fell heavily again last night. The children are delighted because they say we shall soon be obliged to go out by the windows. It is a fact that this morning the front door is blocked and the only way out is by the washhouse. Yesterday I made sure the village was sufficiently provisioned, for we shall doubtless remain cut off from the rest of the world for some time to come. This is not the first winter we have been snowbound, but I cannot remember ever having seen so thick a fall. I take advantage of it to go on with the tale I began yesterday.

I have said that when I first brought home this afflicted child I had not clearly thought out what place she would take in our household. I knew the limits of my wife's powers of endurance; I knew the size of our house and the smallness of our income. I had acted, as usual, in the way that was natural to me, quite as much as on principle, and without for a moment calculating the expense into which my impulse might land me—a proceeding I have always thought contrary to the Gospels' teaching. But it is one thing to trust one's cares to God and quite another to shift them onto other people. I soon saw I had laid a heavy burden on Amélie's shoulders—so heavy that at first I felt struck with shame.

I helped her as best I could to cut the little girl's hair, and I saw that she did even that with disgust. But when it came to washing and cleaning her, I was obliged to leave it to my wife; and I realized that I perforce escaped the heaviest and most disagreeable tasks.

For the rest, Amélie ceased to make the slightest objection. She seemed to have thought things over during the night and resigned herself to her new duties; she even seemed to take some pleasure in them and I saw her smile when she had finished washing and dressing Gertrude. After her head had been shaved and I had rubbed it with ointment, a white cap was put on her; some of Sarah's old clothes and some clean linen took the place of the wretched rags Amélie threw into the fire. The name of Gertrude was chosen by Charlotte and immediately adopted by us all, in our ignorance of her real name, which the orphan girl herself was unaware of, and which I did not know how to find out. She must have been a little younger than Sarah, whose last year's clothes fitted her.

I must here confess the profound and overwhelming disappointment I felt during the first days. I had certainly built up a whole romance for myself on the subject of Gertrude's education, and the reality was a cruel disillusion. The indifference, the apathy of her countenance, or rather its total lack of expression froze my good intentions at their very source. She sat all day long by the fireside, seemingly on the defensive, and as soon as she heard our voices, still more when we came near her, her features appeared to harden; from being expressionless they became hostile; if anyone tried to attract her attention, she began to groan and grunt like an animal. This sulkiness only left her at meal times. I helped her myself and she flung herself on her food with a kind of bestial avidity that was most distressing to witness. And as love responds to love, so a feeling of aversion crept over me at this obstinate withholding of her soul. Yes truly, I confess that at the end of the first ten days I had begun to despair, and my interest in her was even so far diminished that I almost regretted my first impulse and wished I had never brought her home with me. And the absurd thing was that Amélie, being not unnaturally a little triumphant over feelings I was really unable to hide from her, seemed all the more lavish of care and kindness now that she saw Gertrude was becoming a burden to me, and that I felt her presence among us as a mortification.

This was how matters stood when I received a visit from my friend Dr. Martins, of Val Travers, in the course of one of his rounds. He was very much interested by what I told him of Gertrude's condition and was at first greatly astonished she should be so backward, considering her only infirmity was blindness; but I explained that in addition to this she had had to suffer from the deafness of the old woman who was her sole guardian, and who never spoke to her, so that the poor child had been utterly neglected. He persuaded me that in that case I was wrong to despair, but that I was not employing the proper method.

"You are trying to build," he said, "before making sure of your foundations. You must reflect that her whole mind is in a state of chaos and that even its first lineaments are as yet unformed. The first thing to be done is to make her connect together one or two sensations of touch and taste and attach a sound to them—a word—to serve as a kind of label. This you must repeat over and over again indefatigably and then try to get her to say it after you.

"Above all, don't go too quickly; take her at regular hours and never for very long at a time. . . .

"For the rest, this method," he added, after having described it to me minutely, "has nothing particularly magic about it. I did not invent it and other people have applied it. Don't you remember in the philosophy class at school, our professors told us of an analogous case apropos of Condillac and his animated statue—unless," he corrected himself, "I read it later in a psychological review. . . . Never mind; I was much struck by it and I even remember the name of the poor girl, who was still more afflicted than Gertrude, for she was a deafmute as well as blind. She was discovered somewhere in England toward the middle of last century by a doctor who devoted himself to educating her. Her name was Laura Bridgman. The doctor kept a journal, as you ought to do, of the child's progress —or rather, in the first place, of his efforts to instruct her. For days and weeks he went on, first making her feel alternately two little objects, a pin and a pen, and then putting her fingers on the two words *pin* and *pen* printed in a Braille book for the blind. For weeks and weeks there was no result. Her body seemed quite vacant. He did not lose courage, however. 'I felt like a person,' says he, 'leaning over the edge of a deep dark well and desperately dangling a rope in the hope that a hand would catch hold of it.' For he did not for one moment doubt that someone was there at the bottom of the well and that in the end the rope would be caught hold of. And one day, at last, he saw Laura's impassive face light up with a kind of smile. I can well believe that tears of love and gratitude sprang to his eyes and that he straightway fell on his knees and gave thanks to God. Laura had understood at last what it was the doctor wanted. She was saved! From that day forward she was all attention; her progress was rapid; she was soon able to learn by herself and eventually became the head of an institution for the blind—unless that was some other person—for there have been other cases recently that the reviews and newspapers have been full of; they were all astonished—rather foolishly, in my opinion—that such creatures should be happy. For it is a fact that all these walled-up prisoners were happy, and as soon as they were able to express anything, it was their *happiness* they spoke of. The journalists of course went into ecstasies and pointed the 'moral' for people who 'enjoy' all their five senses and yet have the audacity to complain. . . ."

Here an argument arose between Martins and

me, for I objected to his pessimism and could not allow what he seemed to infer—that our senses serve in the long run only to make us miserable.

"That's not what I meant," he protested; "I merely wanted to say, first, that man's spirit imagines beauty, comfort, and harmony more easily and gladly than it can the disorder and sin that everywhere tarnish, stain, degrade, and mar this world; and further, that this state of things is revealed to us by our five senses, which also help us to contribute to it. So that I feel inclined to put the words *si sua mala nescient* after Virgil's *'Fortunatos nimium,'* instead of *'si sua bona norint'* as we are taught. How happy men would be if they knew nothing of evil!"

Then he told me of one of Dickens's stories—which he thinks was directly inspired by Laura Bridgman's case; he promised to send it to me, and four days later I received *The Cricket on the Hearth*, which I read with the greatest pleasure. It is a rather lengthy but at times very touching tale of a little blind girl, maintained by her father, a poor toymaker, in an illusory world of comfort, wealth, and happiness. Dickens exerts all his art in representing this deception as an act of piety, but, thank Heaven, I shall not have to make use of any such falsehood with Gertrude.

The day after Martins's visit I began to put his method into practice with all the application I was capable of. I am sorry now I did not take notes, as he advised, of Gertrude's first steps along the twilit path where I myself at first was but a groping guide. During the first weeks more patience was needed than can well be believed, not only because of the amount of time an education of this kind requires, but also because of the reproaches it brought me. It is painful for me to have to say that these reproaches came from Amélie; but, for that matter, if I mention this here it is because it has not left in me the slightest trace of animosity or bitterness—I declare this most solemnly, in case these lines should come to her eyes later on. (Does not Christ's teaching of the forgiveness of injuries follow immediately after the parable of the lost sheep?) More than that—at the very moment when I most suffered from her reproaches, I could not feel angry with her for disapproving the length of time I devoted to Gertrude. What I chiefly deplored was that she failed to believe that my efforts would be at all successful. Yes, it was her want of faith that grieved me—without, however, discouraging me. How often I heard her repeat: "If only any good were to come of it all! . . ." And she remained stubbornly convinced that my work was labor lost; so that naturally she thought it wrong of me to devote the time to Gertrude's education which she always declared would have been better employed otherwise. And whenever I was occupied with Gertrude, she managed to make out that I was wanted at that moment for someone or something else, and that I was giving her time that ought to have been given to others. In fact, I think she felt a kind of maternal jealousy, for she more than once said to me: "You never took so much pains with any of your own children"—which was true; for though I am very fond of my children, I have never thought it my business to take much pains with them.

It has often been my experience that the parable of the lost sheep is one of the most difficult of acceptance for certain people, who yet believe themselves to be profoundly Christian at heart. That each single sheep of the flock should be in turn more precious in the eyes of the shepherd than the rest of the flock as a whole is beyond and above their power of conception. And the words: "If a man have a hundred sheep and one of them be gone astray, doth he not leave the ninety and nine and goeth into the mountains and seeketh that which is gone astray?"—words all aglow with charity, such persons would, if they dared speak frankly, declare to be abominably unjust.

Gertrude's first smiles consoled me for everything and repaid me for my pains a hundredfold. For "and if so be that he find it, verily I say unto you, he rejoiceth more of that sheep than of the ninety and nine which went not astray." Yes, verily, the smile that dawned for me one morning on that marble face of hers, when she seemed suddenly touched to understanding and interest by what I had been trying for so many days to teach her, flooded my heart with a more seraphic joy than was ever given me by any child of my own.

5 March

I noted this date as if it had been a birthday. It was not so much a smile as a transfiguration. Her features flashed into life—a sudden illumination, like the crimson glow that precedes dawn in the high Alps, thrilling the snowy peak on which it lights and calling it up out of darkness—such a flood it seemed, of mystic color; and I thought too of the pool of Bethesda at the moment the angel descends to stir the slumbering water. A kind of ecstasy rapt me at sight of the angelic expression that came over Gertrude's face so suddenly, for it was clear to me that this heavenly visitor was not so much intelligence as love. And in a very trans-

port of gratitude I kissed her forehead and felt that
I was offering thanks to God.

The progress she made after this was as rapid as
the first steps had been slow. It is only with an
effort that I can now recall our manner of proceeding; it seemed to me sometimes that Gertrude advanced by leaps and bounds, as though in defiance
of all method. I can remember that at first I dwelt
more on the qualities of objects than on their vari-
ety—hot, cold, sweet, bitter, rough, soft, light—
and then on actions: to pick up, to put down, to
remove, to approach, to tie, to cross, to assemble,
to disperse, etc. And very soon I abandoned all
attempt at method and began to talk to her without troubling much whether her mind was always
able to follow me; but I went slowly, inviting and
provoking her questions as she seemed inclined. Certainly her mind was at work during the hours I left
her to herself; for every time I came back to her
after an absence, it was to find with fresh surprise
that the wall of darkness that separated us had
grown less thick. After all, I said to myself, it is so
that the warmth of the air and the insistence of
spring gradually triumph over winter. How often
have I wondered at the melting of the snow! Its
white cloak seems to wear thin from underneath,

while to all appearance it remains unchanged. Every winter Amélie falls into the trap: "The snow is as thick as ever," she declares. And indeed it still seems so, when all at once there comes a break and suddenly, in patches here and there, life once more shows through.

Fearing that Gertrude might become peaky if she continued to sit beside the fire like an old woman, I had begun to make her go out. But she refused to do this unless she held my arm. I realized from her surprise and fear when she first left the house, and before she was able to tell me so in words, that she had never as yet ventured out of doors. In the cottage where I had found her no one had cared for her further than to give her food and prevent her from dying—for I cannot say that anyone helped her to live. Her little universe of darkness was bounded by the walls of the single room she never left; she scarcely ventured on summer days as far as the threshold, when the door stood open to the great universe of light. She told me later that when she heard the birds' song she used to suppose it was simply the effect of light, like the gentle warmth which she felt on her cheeks and hands, and that, without precisely thinking about it, it seemed to her quite natural that the warm air should begin to sing, just as the water begins to boil on the fire.

The truth is she did not trouble to think; she took no interest in anything and lived in a state of frozen numbness till the day I took charge of her. I remember her inexhaustible delight when I told her that the little voices came from living creatures, whose sole function apparently was to express the joy that lies broadcast throughout all nature. (It was from that day that she began to say: "I am as joyful as a bird.") And yet the idea that these songs proclaim the splendor of a spectacle she could not behold had begun by making her melancholy.

"Is the world really as beautiful as the birds say?" she would ask. "Why do people not tell us so oftener? Why do *you* never tell me so? Is it for fear of grieving me because I cannot see it? That would be wrong. I listen so attentively to the birds; I think I understand everything they say."

"People who can see do not hear them as well as you do, my Gertrude," I said, hoping to comfort her.

"Why don't other animals sing?" she went on. Sometimes her questions surprised me and left me perplexed for a moment, for she forced me to reflect on things I had hitherto taken for granted. It was thus it occurred to me for the first time that the closer an animal lives to the ground and the heavier its weight, the duller it is. I tried to make her understand this; and I told her of the squirrel and its gambols.

She asked me if the birds were the only animals that flew.

"There are butterflies too," I told her.

"And do they sing?"

"They have another way of telling their joy. It is painted on their wings. . . ." And I described the rainbow colors of the butterfly.

28 February

Now let me turn back a little, for yesterday I allowed myself to be carried away.

In order to teach Gertrude, I had had to learn the Braille alphabet myself; but she was soon able to read much quicker than I could; I had some difficulty in deciphering the writing, and besides found it easier to follow with my eyes than with my fingers. For that matter, I was not the only one to give her lessons. And at first I was glad to be helped in this respect, for I have a great deal to do in the parish, the houses being so widely scattered that my visits to the poor and the sick sometimes oblige me to go far afield. Jacques had managed to break his arm while skating during the Christmas holidays, which he was spending with us; for during term time he

goes to Lausanne, where he received his early education, and where he is studying at the theological
school. The fracture was not serious and Martins,
whom I at once sent for, was easily able to set it
without the help of a surgeon; but it was considered
advisable for Jacques to keep indoors for some time.
He now suddenly began to take an interest in Gertrude, to whom he had hitherto paid no attention,
and occupied himself with helping me to teach her
to read. His assistance only lasted the time of his
convalescence—about three weeks—but during
those weeks Gertrude's progress was very marked.
She was now fired with extraordinary zeal. Her
young intelligence, but yesterday so benumbed and
torpid, its first steps hardly taken, and scarcely able
to walk, seemed now already preparing to run. I
wondered at the ease with which she succeeded in
formulating her thoughts and at the rapidity with
which she learned to express herself—not childishly, but at once correctly, conveying her ideas by
the help of images, taken in the most delightful and
unexpected way from the objects we had just taught
her to recognize, or from others we described to
her, when we could not actually put them within
her grasp; for she always used things she could
touch or feel in order to explain what was beyond

her reach, after the method of land-surveyors measuring distances.

But I think it is unnecessary to note here all the first steps of her education, doubtless the same in the early education of all blind people. I suppose too that in each case the teacher must have been plunged into a similar perplexity by the question of colors. (And this subject led me to the reflection that there is nowhere any mention of colors in the Gospels.) I do not know how other people set about it; for my part, I began by naming the colors of the prism to her in the order in which they occur in the rainbow; but then a confusion was immediately set up in her mind between color and brightness; and I realized that her imagination was unable to draw any distinction between the *quality* of the shade and what painters, I believe, call its *"value."* She had the greatest difficulty in understanding that every color in its turn might be more or less dark and that they might be mixed one with another to an unlimited extent. It puzzled her exceedingly, and she came back to the subject again and again.

About this time the opportunity was given me of taking her to a concert at Neuchâtel. The part played by each instrument in the symphony suggested to me the idea of recurring to this question of colors. I bade Gertrude observe the different resonances of the brasses, the strings, and the wood instruments, and that each of them was able in its own way to produce the whole series of sounds, from the lowest to the highest, with varying intensity. I asked her to imagine the colors of nature in the same way—the reds and oranges analogous to the sounds of the horns and trombones; the yellows and greens like those of the violins, cellos, and double basses; the violets and blues suggested by the clarinets and oboes. A sort of inner rapture now took the place of all her doubts and uncertainties.

"How beautiful it must be!" she kept on repeating.

Then suddenly she added: "But the white? I can't understand now what the white can be like."

And I at once saw how insecure my comparison was.

"White," I tried however to explain, "is the extreme treble limit where all the tones are blended into one, just as black is the bass or dark limit."

But this did not satisfy me any more than it did her; and she pointed out at once that the wood instruments, the brasses, and the violins remain distinct in the bass as well as in the treble parts. How often I have been obliged to remain puzzled and silent, as I did then, searching about for some comparison I might appeal to.

"Well," said I at last, "imagine white as something absolutely pure, something in which color no longer exists, but only light; and black, on the contrary, something so full of color that it has become dark. . . ."

I recall this fragment of dialogue merely as an example of the difficulties I encountered only too often. Gertrude had this good point, that she never pretended to understand, as people so often do, thus filling their minds with inaccurate or false statements, which in the end vitiate all their reasoning. So long as she could not form a clear idea of any notion, it remained a cause of anxiety and discomfort to her.

As regards what I have just related, the difficulty was increased by the fact that the notion of light and that of heat began by being closely associated with each other in her mind, and I had the greatest trouble afterward in disconnecting them.

Thus, through these experiments with her, it was constantly brought home to me how greatly the visual world differs from the world of sound, and that any comparison between the two must necessarily be a lame one.

I have been so full of my comparisons that I have not yet said what immense pleasure the Neuchâtel concert gave Gertrude. It was actually the *Pastoral Symphony* that was being played. I say *actually* because, as will be easily understood, there is no work I could have more wished her to hear. For a long time after we had left the concert-room, Gertrude remained silent, as though lost in ecstasy.

"Is what you see really as beautiful as that?" she asked at last.

"As beautiful as what, dear child?"

"As that 'scene on the bank of a stream'?"

I did not answer at once, for I was reflecting that those ineffable harmonies painted the world as it might have been, as it would be without evil and without sin, rather than the world as it really was. And I had never yet ventured to speak to Gertrude of evil and sin and death.

"Those who have eyes," I said at last, "do not know their happiness."

"But I who have not," she cried, "*I* know the happiness of hearing."

She pressed up against me as she walked and hung on to my arm in the way small children do.

"Pastor, do you feel how happy I am? No, no, I don't say so to please you. Look at me. Can't you see on people's faces whether they are speaking the truth? I always know by their voices. Do you remember the day you answered me that you weren't crying when my aunt" (that is what she called my wife) "had reproached you with being no help to her? And I cried out: 'Pastor, that's not true!' Oh, I felt at once from your voice that you weren't telling me the truth; there was no need for me to feel your cheeks to know that you had been crying." And she repeated very loud: "No, there was no need for me to feel your cheeks"—which made me turn red, for we were still in the town and the passers-by turned round to look at us. She went on, however:

"You mustn't try to deceive me, you know. First of all, because it would be very mean to try to deceive a blind person . . . and then because you wouldn't succeed," she added, laughing. "Tell me, pastor, you aren't unhappy, are you?"

I put her hand to my lips, as though to make her feel, without having to confess it, that part of my happiness came from her, and answered as I did so.

"No, Gertrude, I am not unhappy. How should I be unhappy?"

"And yet you cry sometimes?"

"I have cried sometimes."

"Not since that time?"

"No, I have not cried again since then."

"And you have not felt inclined to cry?"

"No, Gertrude."

"And tell me—have you felt inclined since then not to speak the truth to me?"

"No, dear child."

"Can you promise never to try to deceive me?"

"I promise."

"Well, tell me quickly, then—am I pretty?"

This sudden question dumbfounded me, all the more because I had studiously avoided up to then taking any notice of Gertrude's undeniable beauty; and moreover I considered it perfectly unnecessary that she should be informed of it herself.

"What can it matter to you?" I said.

"I am anxious," she went on, "I should like to know whether I do not—how shall I put it?—make too much of a discord in the symphony. Whom else should I ask, pastor?"

"It is not a pastor's business to concern himself with the beauty of people's faces," said I, defending myself as best I could.

"Why not?"

"Because the beauty of their souls suffices him."

"You had rather I thought myself ugly," was her

reply with a charming pout; so that, giving up the
struggle, I exclaimed:

"Gertrude, you know quite well you are pretty."

She was silent and her face took on an expression
of great gravity, which did not leave her until we
got home.

On our return Amélie at once managed to make
me feel she disapproved of the way I had been
spending my day. She might have told me so before; but she had let Gertrude and me start without a word, according to her habit of letting people
do things and of reserving to herself the right to
blame them afterward. For that matter, she did
not actually reproach me; but her very silence was
accusing; for surely it would have been natural to
have inquired what we had heard, since she knew I
was taking Gertrude to the concert. Would not the
child's pleasure have been increased if she had felt
that the smallest interest had been taken in it?
But Amélie did not remain entirely silent—she
merely seemed to put a sort of affectation into avoid-
ing any but the most indifferent topics; and it was
not till evening, when the little ones had gone to
bed, and after I had asked her in private and with
some severity if she was vexed with me for taking

Gertrude to the concert, that I got the following answer:

"You do things for her you would never have done for any of your own children."

So it was always the same grievance, and the same refusal to understand that the feast is prepared for the child who returns to us, not for those who have stayed at home, as the parable shows us. It grieved me too to see that she took no account of Gertrude's infirmity—poor Gertrude, who could hope for no other kind of pleasure. And if I providentially happened to be free that afternoon—I, who am as a rule so much in request—Amélie's reproach was all the more unfair, because she knew perfectly well that the other children were busy or occupied in one way or other, and that she herself did not care for music, so that even if she had all the time in the world, it would never enter her head to go to a concert, not even if it were given at our very door.

What distressed me still more was that Amélie had actually said this in front of Gertrude; for though I had taken my wife on one side, she had raised her voice so much that Gertrude heard her. I felt not so much sad as indignant, and a few moments later, when Amélie had left us, I went up to Gertrude and, taking her frail little hand in mine, I lifted it to my face. "You see," I said, "this time I am not crying."

"No," answered she, trying to smile, "this time it is my turn." And as she looked up at me, I suddenly saw her face was flooded with tears.

8 March

The only pleasure I can give Amélie is to refrain from doing the things she dislikes. These very negative signs of love are the only ones she allows me. The degree to which she has already narrowed my life is a thing she cannot realize. Oh, would to Heaven she would demand something difficult of me! How gladly I would undertake a rash, a dangerous task for her! But she seems to have a repugnance for everything that is not usual; so that for her, progress in life consists merely in adding like days to like days. She does not desire—she will not even accept—any new virtue, nor even an increase of the old ones. When it is not with disapproval, it is with mistrust that she views every effort of the soul to find in Christianity something other than the domestication of our instincts.

I must confess that I entirely forgot, that afternoon at Neuchâtel, to go and pay our haberdasher's bill and to bring her back some spools of thread she wanted. But I was more vexed with myself for this than she could have been; especially as I had been quite determined not to forget her commissions, being very well aware that "he that is faithful in that which is least is faithful also in much," and being afraid too of the conclusions she might draw from my forgetfulness. I should even have been glad if she had reproached me with it, for I certainly deserved reproaches. But, as often happens, the imaginary grievance outweighed the definite charge. Ah, how beautiful life would be and how bearable our wretchedness if we were content with real evils without opening the doors to the phantoms and monsters of our imagination! . . . But I am straying here into observations that would do better as the subject of a sermon (Luke xii, 29: "Neither be ye of doubtful mind"). It is the history of Gertrude's intellectual and moral development that I purposed tracing here and I must now return to it.

I had hoped to follow its course step by step in this book and had begun to tell the story in detail. Not only, however, do I lack time to note all its phases with minuteness, but I find it extremely difficult at the present moment to remember their exact sequence. Carried away by my tale, I began by setting down remarks of Gertrude's and conversations with her that are far more recent; a person reading these pages would no doubt be astonished at hearing her express herself so justly and reason so judiciously in such a little while. The fact is her progress was amazingly rapid; I often wondered at the promptness with which her mind fastened on the intellectual food I offered it, and indeed on everything it could catch hold of, absorbing it all by a constant process of assimilation and maturation. The way in which she forestalled my thoughts and outstripped them was a continual surprise to me, and often from one lesson to another I ceased to recognize my pupil.

At the end of a very few months there was no appearance of her intelligence having lain dormant for so long. Even at this early stage she showed more sense and judgment than the generality of young girls, distracted as they are by the outside world and prevented from giving their best attention by a multitude of futile preoccupations. She was moreover a good deal older, I think, than we had at first supposed. Indeed, it seemed as though she were determined to profit by her blindness, so that I actually wondered whether this infirmity was not in many ways an advantage. In spite of myself I compared her with Charlotte, so easily distracted by the veriest trifles, so that many a time while hearing the child say over her lessons, as I sometimes did, I found myself thinking: "Dear me, how much better she would listen if only she could not see!"

Needless to say, Gertrude was a very eager reader, but as I wished as far as possible to keep in touch with the development of her mind, I preferred her not to read too much—or at any rate not much without me—and especially not the Bible—which may seem very strange for a Protestant. I will explain myself; but before touching on a question so important, I wish to relate a small circumstance that is connected with music and should be placed, as far as I can remember, shortly after the concert at Neuchâtel.

Yes, the concert, I think, took place three weeks before the summer vacation, which brought Jacques home. In the meantime I had often sat with Gertrude at the little harmonium of our chapel, which is usually played by Mlle de la M., with whom Gertrude is at present staying. Louise de la M. had not yet begun to give Gertrude music lessons. Notwithstanding my love for music, I do not know much about it, and I felt very little able to teach her anything when I sat beside her at the keyboard.

"No," she had said after the first gropings, "you had better leave me. I had rather try by myself."

And I left her all the more willingly that the chapel did not seem to me a proper place in which to be shut up alone with her, as much out of respect for the sanctity of the place as for fear of gossip—though as a rule I endeavor to disregard it; in this case, however, it is a matter that concerns not only me but her. So when a round of visits called me in that direction, I would take her to the church and leave her there, often for long hours together, and then would go to fetch her on my return. In this way she spent her time patiently hunting out harmonies, and I would find her again toward evening pondering over some concord of sounds that had plunged her into a long ecstasy.

On one of the first days of August, barely more than six months ago, it so happened that I had gone to visit a poor widow in need of consolation and had not found her in. I therefore returned at once to fetch Gertrude from the church, where I had left her; she was not expecting me back so soon, and I was extremely surprised to find Jacques with her. Neither of them heard me come in, for the little noise I made was covered by the sound of the organ. It is not in my nature to play the spy, but everything that touches Gertrude touches me; so stepping as softly as I could, I stole up the few steps that lead to the gallery—an excellent post of observation. I must say that during the whole time I was there I did not hear a word from either of them that they might not have said before me. But he sat very close to her, and several times I saw him take her hand in order to guide her fingers over the keys. Was it not in itself strange that she should accept instructions and guidance from him when she had previously refused them from me, preferring, she said, to practice by herself? I was more astonished, more pained, than I liked to own and was just on the point of intervening when I saw Jacques suddenly take out his watch.

"I must leave you now," he said; "my father will be coming back in a moment."

I saw him lift her unresisting hand to his lips; then he left. A few moments later I went noiselessly down the stairs and opened the church door so that she might hear me and think I had only just arrived.

"Well, Gertrude! Are you ready to go home? How is the organ getting on?"

"Very well," she answered in the most natural tone; "I have really made some progress today."

A great sadness filled my heart, but we neither of us made any allusion to the episode I have just described.

I was impatient to find myself alone with Jacques. My wife, Gertrude, and the children used as a rule to go to bed rather early after supper, while we two sat on late over our studies. I was waiting for this moment. But before speaking to him I felt my heart bursting with such a mixture of feelings that I could not—or dared not—begin on the subject that was tormenting me. And it was he who abruptly broke the silence by announcing his intention of spending the rest of the vacation with us. Now, a few days earlier he had spoken to us about a tour he wanted to make in the high Alps —a plan my wife and I heartily approved of; I knew his friend T., who was to be his traveling companion, was counting on him; it was therefore quite obvious to me that this sudden change of plan was not unconnected with the scene I had just come upon. I was at first stirred by violent indignation, but was afraid to give way to it lest it should put an end to my son's confidence altogether; I was afraid too of pronouncing words I should afterward regret; so making a great effort over myself, I said as naturally as I could:

"I thought T. was counting on you."

"Oh," he answered, "not absolutely, and besides he will have no difficulty in finding someone else to go with him. I can rest here quite as well as in the Oberland, and I really think I can spend my time better than mountaineering."

"In fact," I said, "you have found something to occupy you at home."

He noticed some irony in the tone of my voice and looked at me, but being unable as yet to guess the motive of it, went on unconcernedly:

"You know I have always liked reading better than climbing."

"Yes, my dear boy," said I, returning his glance with one as searching; "but are not lessons in harmonium-playing even more attractive than reading?"

No doubt he felt himself blush, for he put his hand to his forehead, as though to shade his eyes from the lamplight; but he recovered himself almost immediately and went on in a voice I could have wished less steady:

"Do not blame me too much, Father. I did not mean to hide anything from you and you have only forestalled by a very little the confession I was preparing to make you."

He spoke deliberately, as if he were reading the words out of a book, finishing his sentences with as much calm, it seemed, as if it were a matter in which he had no concern. The extraordinary self-possession he showed brought my exasperation to a climax. Feeling that I was about to interrupt him, he raised his hand, as much as to say: "No, you can speak afterward; let me finish first." But I seized his arm and shook it.

"Oh," I exclaimed impetuously, "I would rather never see you again than have you trouble the purity of Gertrude's soul. I don't want your confessions! To abuse infirmity, innocence, candor—what abominable cowardice! I should never have thought you capable of it. And to speak of it with such cold-blooded unconcern! . . . Understand me: it is I who have charge of Gertrude and I will not suffer you to speak to her, to touch her, to see her for one single day more."

"But, Father," he went on as calmly as ever, driving me almost beside myself, "you may be sure that I respect Gertrude as much as you can. You are making a strange mistake if you think there is anything reprehensible—I don't say in my conduct, but in my intentions and in my secret heart. I love Gertrude and respect her, I tell you, as much as I love her. The idea of troubling her, of abusing her innocence, is as abominable to me as to you."

Then he protested that what he wanted was to be her help, her friend, her husband; that he had thought he ought not to speak to me about it until he had made up his mind to marry her; that Gertrude herself did not know of his intention and that he had wanted to speak to me about it first.

"This is the confession I had to make to you," he wound up; "and I have nothing else to confess, believe me."

These words filled me with stupor. As I listened, I felt my temples throbbing. I had been prepared with nothing but reproaches, and the fewer grounds he gave me for indignation, the more at a loss I felt, so that at the end of his speech I had nothing left to say.

"Let us go to bed," I said at last, after some moments of silence. I got up and put my hand on his shoulder. "Tomorrow I will tell you what I think about it all."

"Tell me at any rate that you aren't still angry with me."

"I must have the night to think it over."

When I saw Jacques again the next morning, I seemed to be looking at him for the first time. I suddenly realized that my son was no longer a child but a young man; so long as I thought of him as a child, the love that I had accidentally discovered might appear monstrous. I had passed the whole night persuading myself that on the contrary it was perfectly natural and normal. Why was it that my dissatisfaction only became keener still? It was not till later that this became clear to me. In the meantime I had to speak to Jacques and tell him my decision. Now an instinct as sure as the voice of conscience warned me that this marriage must be prevented at all costs.

I took Jacques down to the bottom of the garden.

"Have you said anything to Gertrude?" I began by asking him.

"No," he answered; "perhaps she feels I love her, but I have not yet told her so."

"Then you must promise me not to speak of it yet awhile."

"I am determined to obey you, Father; but may I not know your reasons?"

I hesitated to give them, feeling doubtful whether those that first came into my mind were the wisest to put forward. To tell the truth, conscience rather than reason dictated my conduct.

"Gertrude is too young," I said at last. "You must reflect that she has not yet been confirmed. You know she was unhappily not like other children and did not begin to develop till very late. She is so trustful that she would no doubt be only too easily touched by the first words of love she heard; that is why it is of importance not to say them. To take possession of what is defenseless is cowardice;

I know that you are not a coward. Your feelings,
you say, are in no way reprehensible; I say they
are wrong because they are premature. It is our duty
to be prudent for Gertrude till she is able to be
prudent for herself. It is a matter of conscience."

Jacques has one excellent point—that the simple
words I often used to him as a child: "I appeal to
your conscience," have always been sufficient to
check him. Meanwhile, as I looked at him, I
thought that if Gertrude were able to see, she could
not fail to admire the tall slender figure, so straight
and yet so lithe, the smooth forehead, the frank
look, the face, so childlike still, though now, as it
were, overshadowed by a sudden gravity. He was
bareheaded, and his fair hair, which was rather
long at that time, curled a little at the temples and
half hid his ears.

"There is another thing I want to ask you," I
went on, rising from the bench where we had been
sitting. "You had intended, you said, to go away
the day after tomorrow; I beg you not to put off
your leaving. You were to remain away a whole
month at least; I beg you not to shorten your absence by a single day. Is that agreed?"

"Very well, Father, I will obey."

I thought he turned extremely pale—so pale that
the color left even his lips. But I persuaded myself

that such prompt submission argued no very great love, and I felt inexpressibly relieved. I was touched besides by his obedience.

"That's the child I love," I said gently. And drawing him to me, I put my lips to his forehead. There was a slight recoil on his part, but I refused to feel hurt by it.

10 March

Our house is so small that we are obliged to live more or less on top of one another, which is sometimes very inconvenient for my work, although I keep a little room for myself upstairs where I can receive my visitors in private—and especially inconvenient when I want to speak to one of the family in private, without such an air of solemnity as would be the case if the interview took place in this little parlor of mine, which the children call my "sanctum" and into which they are forbidden to enter. On that particular morning, however, Jacques had gone to Neuchâtel to buy a pair of boots for his mountaineering, and as it was very fine, the children had gone out after lunch with Gertrude, whom they take charge of, while she at the same time takes charge of them. (It is a pleasure for me to note that Charlotte is particularly attentive to

her.) At tea, then, a meal we always take in the
common sitting-room, I was quite naturally left
alone with Amélie. This was just what I wanted, for
I was longing to speak to her. It happens to me so
rarely to have a tête-à-tête with her, that I felt
almost shy, and the importance of what I had to
say agitated me as much as if it had been a question, not of Jacques's affairs, but of my own. I felt
too, before I began to speak, how two people who
love each other and live practically the same life
can yet remain (or become) as much of an enigma
to each other as if they lived behind stone walls.
Words in this case—those spoken or those heard—
have the pathetic sound of vain knocking against
the resistance of that dividing barrier, which, unless watch be kept, will grow more and more impenetrable. . . .

"Jacques was speaking to me last night and again
this morning," I began as she poured out the tea;
and my voice was as faltering as Jacques's had been
steady the day before. "He told me he loved Gertrude."

"It was quite right of him to tell you," said she
without looking at me and continuing her house-
wifely task, as if I had said the most natural thing
in the world—or rather as if I had said nothing she
did not already know.

"He told me he wanted to marry her; he is resolved to—"

"It was only to be expected," she murmured with a slight shrug of her shoulders.

"Then you suspected it?" I asked in some vexation.

"I've seen it coming on for a long while. But that's the kind of thing men never notice."

It would have been no use to protest, and besides there was perhaps some truth in her rejoinder, so "In that case," I simply objected, "you might have warned me."

She gave me the little crooked smile with which she sometimes accompanies and screens her reticences, and then, with a sideways nod of her head, "If I had to warn you," she said, "of everything you can't see for yourself, I should have my work cut out for me!"

What did she mean by this insinuation? I did not know or care to know, and went on, without attending to it:

"Well, but I want to hear what you think about it."

She sighed. Then: "You know, my dear, that I never approved of that child's staying with us."

I found it difficult not to be irritated by her harking back in this way to the past.

"Gertrude's staying with us is not what we are discussing," I said, but Amélie went on:

"I have always thought it would lead to no good."

With a strong desire to be conciliatory, I caught at her phrase:

"Then you think it would be no good if it led to such a marriage? That's just what I wanted to hear you say. I am glad we are of the same opinion." Then I added that Jacques had submitted quietly to the reasons I had given him, so that there was no need for her to be anxious; that it had been agreed he was to leave the next day for his trip and stay away a whole month.

"As I have no more wish than you that he should find Gertrude here when he comes back," I wound up, "I think the best thing would be to hand her over to the care of Mademoiselle de la M. and I could continue to see her there; for there's no denying that I have very serious obligations to her. I have just been to sound our friend and she is quite ready to oblige us. In this way you will be rid of a presence that is painful to you. Louise de la M. will look after Gertrude; she seemed delighted with the arrangement; she is looking forward already to giving her harmony lessons."

Amélie seemed determined to remain silent, so that I went on:

"As we shall not want Jacques to see Gertrude there, I think it would be a good thing to warn Mademoiselle de la M. of the state of affairs, don't you?"

I hoped by putting this question to get something out of her; but she kept her lips tightly shut, as if she had sworn not to speak. And I went on—not that I had anything more to add, but because I could not endure her silence:

"For that matter, perhaps Jacques will have got over his love by the time he gets back. At his age one hardly knows what one wants."

"And even later one doesn't always know," said she at last, rather oddly.

Her enigmatical and slightly oracular way of speaking irritated me, for I am too frank by nature to put up easily with mystery-making. Turning toward her, I begged her to explain what she meant to imply by that.

"Nothing, my dear," she answered sadly. "I was only thinking that a moment ago you were wishing to be warned of the things you didn't notice yourself."

"Well?"

"Well, I was thinking that it's not always easy to warn people."

I have said that I hate mysteries and I object on principle to hints and double meanings.

"When you want me to understand you, perhaps you will explain yourself more clearly," I replied, rather brutally, perhaps, and I was sorry as soon as I had said it; for I saw her lips tremble a moment. She turned her head aside, then got up and took a few hesitating, almost tottering steps about the room.

"But, Amélie," I cried, "why do you go on being unhappy now that everything is all right again?"

I felt that my eyes embarrassed her, and it was with my back turned and my elbows on the table, resting my head in my hands, that I went on to say:

"I spoke to you unkindly just now. Forgive me."

At that I heard her come up behind me; then I felt her lay her fingers gently on my head as she said tenderly and in a voice trembling with tears:

"My poor dear!"

Then she left the room quickly.

Amélie's words, which I then thought so mysterious, became clear to me soon after this; I have written them down as they struck me at the moment; and that day I only understood that it was time Gertrude should leave.

12 March

I had imposed on myself the duty of devoting a little time daily to Gertrude—a few hours or a few minutes, according to the occupations in hand. The day after this conversation with Amélie, I had some free time, and as the weather was inviting, I took Gertrude with me through the forest to that fold in the Jura where in the clear weather one can see, through a curtain of branches and across an immense stretch of land at one's feet, the wonder of the snowy Alps emerging from a thin veil of mist. The sun was already declining on the left when we reached our customary seat. A meadow of thick, closely cropped grass sloped downwards at our feet; farther off, a few cows were grazing; each of them among these mountain herds wears a bell at its neck.

"They outline the landscape," said Gertrude as she listened to their tinkling.

She asked me, as she does every time we go for a walk, to describe the place where we had stopped.

"But you know it already," I told her; "on the fringe of the forest, where one can see the Alps."

"Can one see them clearly today?"

"Yes, in all their splendor."

"You told me they were a little different every day."

"What shall I compare them to this afternoon? To a thirsty midsummer's day. Before evening they will have melted into the air."

"I should like you to tell me if there are any lilies in the big meadows before us."

"No, Gertrude, lilies do not grow on these heights, or only a few rare species."

"Not even the lilies called the lilies of the field?"

"There are no lilies in the fields."

"Not even in the fields round Neuchâtel?"

"There are no lilies of the field."

"Then why did our Lord say: 'Consider the lilies of the field'?"

"There were some in his day, no doubt, for him to say so; but they have disappeared before men and their plows."

"I remember you have often told me that what this world most needs is confidence and love. Don't you think that with a little more confidence men would see them again? When I listen to His word, I assure you I see them. I will describe them to you, shall I? They are like bells of flame—great bells of azure, filled with the perfume of love and swinging in the evening breeze. Why do you say there are none there before us? I feel them! I see the meadow filled with them."

"They are not more beautiful than you see them, my Gertrude."

"Say they are not less beautiful."

"They are as beautiful as you see them."

" 'And yet I say unto you that even Solomon in all his glory was not arrayed like one of these,' " said she, quoting Christ's words; and when I heard her melodious voice, I felt I was listening to them for the first time. " 'In all his glory,' " she repeated thoughtfully, and was silent for a time. I went on:

"I have told you, Gertrude, that it is those who have eyes who cannot see." And a prayer rose from the bottom of my heart: "I thank Thee, O Lord, that Thou revealest to the humble what Thou hidest from the wise."

"If you knew," she exclaimed in a rapture of delight, "if you knew how easily I imagine it all! Would you like me to describe the landscape to you? . . . Behind us, above us, and around us are the great fir trees, with their scent of resin and ruddy trunks, stretching out their long dark horizontal branches and groaning as the wind tries to bend them. At our feet, like an open book on the sloping desk of the mountain, lies the broad green meadow, shot with shifting colors—blue in the shade, golden in the sun, and speaking in clear words of flowers—gentians, pulsatillas, ranunculus, and Solomon's beautiful lilies; the cows come and spell them out with their bells; and the angels come and read them—for you say that the eyes of men are closed. Below the book I see a great smoky, misty river of milk, hiding abysses of mystery—an immense river, whose only shore is the beautiful, dazzling Alps far, far away in the distance. . . . That's where Jacques is going. Tell me, is he really starting tomorrow?"

"He is to start tomorrow. Did he tell you so?"

"He didn't tell me so, but I guessed it. Will he be away long?"

"A month. . . . Gertrude, I want to ask you something. Why didn't you tell me that he used to meet you in the church?"

"He came twice. Oh, I don't want to hide anything from you; but I was afraid of making you unhappy."

"It would make me unhappy if you didn't tell me."

Her hand sought mine.

"He was sad at leaving."

"Tell me, Gertrude—did he say he loved you?"

"He didn't say so, but I can feel it without being

told. He doesn't love me as much as you do."

"And you, Gertrude, does it make you unhappy that he should go away?"

"I think it is better he should go. I couldn't respond."

"But tell me, does it make you unhappy that he should go?"

"You know, pastor, that it's you I love. . . . Oh, why do you take your hand away? I shouldn't speak so if you weren't married. But no one marries a blind girl. Then why shouldn't we love each other? Tell me, pastor, do you think there's anything wrong in it?"

"It's never in love that the wrong lies."

"I feel there is nothing but good in my heart. I don't want to make Jacques suffer. I don't want to make anyone suffer. . . . I only want to give happiness."

"Jacques was thinking of asking you to marry him."

"Will you let me speak to him before he goes? I should like to make him understand that he must give up loving me. Pastor, you understand, don't you, that I can't marry anyone? You'll let me speak to him, won't you?"

"This evening."

"No, tomorrow; just before he leaves. . . ."

The sun was setting in majestic splendor. The evening air was warm. We had risen and, talking as we went, we turned back along the somber homeward path.

SECOND NOTEBOOK

I HAVE BEEN obliged to put this book aside for some time.

The snow melted at last and as soon as the roads were passable, there were a great many things to be done that I had been obliged to put off all the long while our village was isolated from the outer world. It was only yesterday I was able for the first time to find a few moments' leisure again.

Last night I read over everything I had written here. . . .

Now that I dare call by its name the feeling that so long lay unacknowledged in my heart, it seems almost incomprehensible that I should have mistaken it until this very day—incomprehensible that those words of Amélie's that I recorded should have appeared mysterious—that even after Gertrude's naïve declarations, I could still have doubted that I loved her. The fact is that I would not then allow that any love outside marriage could be permissi-

ble, nor at the same time would I allow that there
could be anything whatever forbidden in the feeling that drew me so passionately to Gertrude.

The innocence of her avowals, their very frank-
ness, reassured me. I told myself she was only a
child. Real love would not go without confusion
and blushes. As far as I was concerned, I persuaded
myself I loved her as one loves an afflicted child. I
tended her as one tends a sick person—and so I
made a moral obligation, a duty, of what was really
a passionate inclination. Yes, truly, on the very
evening she spoke to me in the way I have described,
so happy was I, so light of heart, that I misunderstood my real feelings, and even as I transcribed our
talk, I misunderstood them still. For I should have
considered love reprehensible, and my conviction
was that everything reprehensible must lie heavy
on the soul; therefore, as I felt no weight on my
soul, I had no thought of love.

These conversations not only were set down just
as they occurred, but were also written while I was
in the same frame of mind as when they took place;
to tell the truth, it was only when I reread them
last night that I understood. . . .

As soon as Jacques had gone (I had allowed Gertrude to speak to him before he left, and when he

returned for the last few days of his vacation, he
affected either to avoid her altogether or to speak to
her only in my presence), our life slipped back into
its usual peaceful course. Gertrude, as had been
arranged, went to stay at Mlle Louise's, where I
visited her every day. But, again in my fear of love,
I made a point of not talking to her of anything
likely to agitate us. I spoke to her only as a pastor
and for the most part in Louise's presence, occu-
pying myself chiefly with her religious instruction
and with preparing her for Holy Communion, which
she has just partaken of this Easter.

I too communicated on Easter Day.

This was a fortnight ago. To my surprise, Jacques,
who was spending a week's holiday with us, did
not accompany us to the Lord's Table. And I
greatly regret having to say that Amélie also ab-
stained—for the first time since our marriage. It
seemed as though the two of them had come to
an understanding and resolved by their abstention
from this solemn celebration to throw a shadow
over my joy. Here again I congratulated myself
that Gertrude could not see and that I was left to
bear the weight of this shadow alone. I know Amélie
too well not to be aware of all the blame she wished
indirectly to convey by her conduct. She never
openly disapproves of me, but she makes a point of

showing her displeasure by leaving me in a sort of isolation.

I was profoundly distressed that a grievance of this kind—such a one, I mean, as I shrink from contemplating—should have so affected Amélie's soul as to turn her aside from her higher interests. And when I came home I prayed for her in all sincerity of heart.

As for Jacques's abstention, it was due to quite another motive, as a conversation I had with him a little later on made clear.

3 May

Gertrude's religious instruction has led me to re-read the Gospels with a fresh eye. It seems to me more and more that many of the notions that constitute our Christian faith originate not from Christ's own words but from St. Paul's commentaries.

This was, in fact, the subject of the discussion I have just had with Jacques. By disposition he is somewhat hard and rigid, and his mind is not sufficiently nourished by his heart; he is becoming traditionalist and dogmatic. He reproaches me with choosing out of the Christian doctrine "what pleases me." But I do not pick and choose among Christ's words. I simply, between Christ and St. Paul, choose Christ. He, on the contrary, for fear of finding them in opposition, refuses to dissociate them, refuses to feel any difference of inspiration between them, and makes objections when I say that in one case it is a man I hear, while in the other it is God. The more he argues, the more persuaded I am he does not feel that Christ's slightest word has a divine accent that is unique.

I search the Gospels, I search in vain for commands, threats, prohibitions. . . . All of these come from St. Paul. And it is precisely because they are not to be found in the words of Christ that Jacques is disturbed. Souls like his think themselves lost as soon as they are deprived of their props, their handrails, their fences. And besides they cannot endure others to enjoy a liberty they have resigned, and want to obtain by compulsion what would readily be granted by love.

"But, Father," he said, "I too desire the soul's happiness."

"No, my friend, you desire its submission."

"It is in submission that happiness lies."

I leave him the last word because I dislike arguing; but I know that happiness is endangered when one seeks to obtain it by what should on the contrary be the effect of happiness—and if it is true that the loving soul rejoices in a willing submission, nothing is farther from happiness than submission without love.

For the rest, Jacques reasons well, and if I were not distressed at seeing so much doctrinal harshness in so young a mind, I should no doubt admire the quality of his arguments and his unbending logic. It often seems to me that I am younger than he is—younger today than I was yesterday—and I repeat to myself the words:

"Except ye become as little children, ye shall not enter into the kingdom of heaven."

Do I betray Christ, do I slight, do I profane the Gospels when I see in them above all a *method for attaining the life of blessedness?* The state of joy, which our doubt and the hardness of our hearts prevent, is an obligation laid upon every Christian. Every living creature is more or less capable of joy. Every living creature ought to tend to joy. Gertrude's smile alone teaches me more in this respect than all my lessons teach her.

And these words of Christ's stood out before my eyes in letters of light: "If ye were blind ye should have no sin." Sin is that which darkens the soul—which prevents its joy. Gertrude's perfect happiness, which shines forth from her whole being,

comes from the fact that she does not know sin.
There is nothing in her but light and love.

I have put into her vigilant hands the four Gospels, the Psalms, the Apocalypse, and the three
Epistles of St. John, so that she may read: "God is
light, and in him is no darkness at all," as in the
Gospel she has already heard the Saviour say: "I
am the light of the world." I will not give her the
Epistles of St. Paul, for if, being blind, she knows
not sin, what is the use of troubling her by letting
her read: "sin by the commandment might become
exceeding sinful" (Romans vii, 13) and the whole
of the dialectic that follows, admirable as it may be.

8 May

Dr. Martins came over yesterday from Chaux-de-
Fonds. He examined Gertrude's eyes for a long
time with the ophthalmoscope. He told me he had
spoken about Gertrude to Dr. Roux, the Lausanne
specialist, and is to report his observations to him.
They both have an idea that Gertrude might be
operated on with success. But we have agreed to say
nothing about it to her as long as things are not
more certain. Martins is to come and let me know
what they think after they have consulted. What

would be the good of raising Gertrude's hopes if
there is any risk of their being immediately extinguished? And besides is she not happy as she
is? . . .

10 May

At Easter Jacques and Gertrude saw each other
again in my presence—at least, Jacques saw Gertrude and spoke to her, but only about trifles. He
seemed less agitated than I feared; and I persuade
myself afresh that if his love had really been very
ardent, he would not have got over it so easily, even
though Gertrude had told him last year before he
went away that it was hopeless. I noticed that he
no longer says "thou" to Gertrude, but calls her
"you" which is certainly preferable; however, I had
not asked him to do so and I am glad it was his
own idea. There is undoubtedly a great deal of good
in him.

I suspect, however, that this submission of
Jacques's was not arrived at without a struggle.
The unfortunate thing is that the constraint he has
been obliged to impose on his feelings now seems to
him good in itself; he would like to see it imposed
on everyone; I felt this in the discussion I had
with him that I have recorded farther back. Is it not

La Rochefoucauld who says that the mind is often the dupe of the heart? I need not say that, knowing Jacques as I do, I did not venture to point this out to him there and then, for I take him to be one of those people who are only made more obstinate by argument; but the very same evening I found what furnished me with a reply—and from St. Paul himself (I could only beat him with his own weapons)—and left a little note in his room, in which I wrote out the text: "Let not him which eateth not judge him that eateth: for God hath received him" (Romans xiv, 3).

I might as well have copied out what follows: "I know, and am persuaded by the Lord Jesus, that there is nothing unclean of itself: but to him that esteemeth any thing to be unclean, to him it is unclean." But I did not dare to, for I was afraid that Jacques might proceed to suspect me of some wrongful interpretation with regard to Gertrude— a suspicion that must not so much as cross his imagination for a second. Evidently it is here a question of food; but in how many passages of the Scriptures are we not called on to give the words a double and triple meaning? ("If thine eye . . ." and the multiplication of the loaves, the miracle of Cana, etc.) This is not a matter of logic-chopping; the meaning of this text is wide and deep: the restriction must not be dictated by the law but by love, and St. Paul exclaims immediately afterward: "But if thy brother be grieved with thy meat, now walkest thou not charitably." It is where love fails that the chink in our armor lies. That is where the Evil One attacks us. Lord, remove from my heart all that does not belong to love. . . . For I was wrong to provoke Jacques: the next morning I found on my table the same note on which I had written out the text; Jacques had simply written on the back of it another text from the same chapter: "Destroy not him with thy meat for whom Christ died" (Romans xiv, 15).

I have reread the whole chapter. It is the starting-point for endless discussion. And is Gertrude to be tormented with these perplexities? Is the brightness of her sky to be darkened with these clouds? Am I not nearer Christ, do I not keep her nearer to Him, when I teach her, when I let her believe, that the only sin is that which hurts the happiness of others or endangers our own?

Alas! There are some souls to whom happiness is uncongenial; they cannot, they do not know how to avail themselves of it. . . . I am thinking of my poor Amélie. I never cease imploring her, urging her—I wish I could force her to be happy. Yes, I wish I could lift everyone up to God. But she will

none of it; she curls up like certain flowers that
never open to the sun. Everything she sees causes
her uneasiness and distress.

"What's the good, my dear?" she answered me
the other day, "we can't all be blind."

Ah, how her irony grieves me! And what courage I need not to be disturbed by it! And yet it
seems to me she ought to understand that this allusion to Gertrude's infirmity is particularly painful
to me. She makes me feel, indeed, that what I admire above all in Gertrude is her infinite mildness;
I have never heard her express the slightest resent-
ment against anyone. It is true I do not allow her
to hear anything that might hurt her.

And as the soul that is happy diffuses happiness
around it by the radiation of love, so everything in
Amélie's neighborhood becomes gloomy and mo-
rose. Amiel would say that her soul gives out black
rays. When, after a harassing day of toil—visits
to the sick, the poor, the afflicted—I come in at
nightfall, tired out and with a heart longing for
rest, affection, warmth, it is to find, more often
than not, worries, recriminations and quarrels,
which I dread a thousand times more than the cold,
the wind, and the rain out of doors. I know well
enough that our old Rosalie invariably wants her
own way, but she is not always in the wrong, nor

Amélie always in the right when she tries to make her give in. I know that Gaspard and Charlotte are horribly unruly; but would not Amélie get better results if she scolded them less loudly and less constantly? So much nagging, so many reprimands and expostulations, lose their edge like pebbles on the seashore; they are far less disturbing to the children than to me. I know that Claude is teething (at least that is what his mother declares every time he sets up a howl), but does it not encourage him to howl for her or Sarah to run and pick him up and be forever petting him? I am convinced he would not howl so often if he was left to howl once or twice to his heart's content when I am not there. But I know that is the very time they spoil him most.

Sarah is like her mother, and for that reason I should have wished to send her to school. She is not, alas, what her mother was at her age, when we were first engaged, but what the material cares of life have made her—I was going to say the *cultivation* of the cares of life, for Amélie certainly does cultivate them. I find it indeed very difficult to recognize in her today the angel of those early times who smiled encouragement on every high-minded impulse of my heart, who I dreamed would be the sharer of my every hope and fear, and whom I looked on as my guide and leader along the path

to heaven—or did love blind me in those days? . . .
I cannot see that Sarah has any interests that are
not vulgar; like her mother, she allows herself to
be entirely taken up with paltry household matters;
the very features of her face, unilluminated as they
are by any inward flame, look dull and almost hard.
She has no taste for poetry or for reading in general; I never overhear any conversation between
her and her mother in which I have any inclination
to take part, and I feel my isolation even more painfully when I am with them than when I retire to
my study, as it is becoming my custom to do more
and more often.

And I have also fallen into the habit this autumn,
encouraged by the shortness of the days, of taking
tea at Mlle de la M.'s whenever my rounds permit
it—that is, whenever I can get back early enough.
I have not yet mentioned that since last November
Louise de la M. has extended her hospitality to three
little blind girls, entrusted to her care by Martins.
Gertrude is teaching them to read and to work at
sundry little tasks over which they have already
begun to be quite clever.

How restful, how comforting I find its warm
friendly atmosphere every time I re-enter the
Grange, and how much I miss it if I am obliged to
let two or three days pass without going there.

Mlle de la M., it is hardly necessary to say, has sufficient means to take in and provide for Gertrude and the three little boarders without putting herself out in any way; three maidservants help her with the greatest devotion and save her all fatigue. Can one imagine fortune and leisure better bestowed? Louise de la M. has always interested herself in the poor; she is a profoundly religious woman and seems hardly to belong to this earth or to live for anything but love; though her hair is already silvery under its lace cap, nothing can be more childlike than her laugh, nothing more harmonious than her movements, nothing more musical than her voice. Gertrude has caught her manners, her way of speaking, almost the intonation, not only of her voice, but of her mind, of her whole being—a likeness upon which I tease them both, but which neither of them will admit. How sweet it is, when I can find the time, to linger in their company, to see them sitting beside each other, Gertrude either leaning her head on her friend's shoulder or clasping one of her hands in hers, while I read them some lines out of Lamartine or Hugo; how sweet to behold the beauties of such poetry reflected in the mirror of their limpid souls! Even the little pupils are touched by it. These children, in this atmosphere of peace and love, develop astonish-

ingly and make remarkable progress. I smiled at
first when Mlle Louise spoke of teaching them to
dance—for their health's sake as much as for their
amusement—but now I admire the rhythmic grace
to which they have attained, though they themselves, alas, are unable to appreciate it. And yet
Louise de la M. has persuaded me that though they
cannot see, they do physically perceive the harmony of their movements. Gertrude takes part in
their dances with the most charming grace and
sweetness, and moreover seems to take the keenest
pleasure in them. Or sometimes it is Louise de la M.
who directs the little girls' movements, and then
Gertrude seats herself at the piano. Her progress
in music has been astonishing; she plays the organ
in chapel now every Sunday and preludes short
improvisations to the singing of the hymns. Every
Sunday she comes to lunch with us; my children are
delighted to see her, notwithstanding that their
tastes are growing more and more divergent. Amélie
is not too irritable and we get through the meal
without a hitch. After lunch the whole family goes
back with Gertrude to the Grange and has tea there.
It is a treat for my children, and Louise enjoys
spoiling them and loading them with delicacies.
Amélie, who is far from being insensible to atten-
tions of this kind, unbends at last and looks ten

years younger. I think she would find it difficult now to do without this halt in the wearisome round of her daily life.

18 May

Now that the fine weather has returned, I have been able to go out again with Gertrude—a thing I had not done for a long time (for there have been fresh falls of snow quite recently and the roads have been in a terrible state until only a few days ago), and it is a long time too since I have found myself alone with her.

We walked quickly; the sharp air colored her cheeks and kept blowing her fair hair over her face. As we passed alongside a peat-bog, I picked one or two rushes that were in flower and slipped their stalks under her béret; then I twined them into her hair so as to keep them in place.

We had scarcely spoken to each other as yet in the astonishment of finding ourselves alone together, when Gertrude turned her sightless face toward me and asked abruptly:

"Do you think Jacques still loves me?"

"He has made up his mind to give you up," I replied at once.

"But do you think he knows you love me?" she went on.

Since the conversation I have related above, more than six months had gone by without (strange to say) the slightest word of love having passed between us. We were never alone, as I have said, and it was better so. . . . Gertrude's question made my heart beat so fast that I was obliged to slacken our pace a little.

"My dear Gertrude, everyone knows I love you," I cried. But she was not to be put off.

"No, no; you have not answered my question."

And after a moment's silence she went on, with lowered head:

"Aunt Amélie knows it; and *I* know it makes her sad."

"She would be sad anyway," I protested with an unsteady voice. "It is her nature to be sad."

"Oh, you always try to reassure me," she answered with some impatience. "But I don't want to be reassured. There are a great many things, I feel sure, you don't tell me about for fear of troubling or grieving me; a great many things I don't know, so that sometimes—"

Her voice dropped lower and lower; she stopped as if for want of breath. And when, taking up her last words, I asked:

"So that sometimes—?"

"So that sometimes," she continued sadly, "I

think all the happiness I owe you is founded upon ignorance."

"But, Gertrude—"

"No, let me say this: I don't want a happiness of that kind. You must understand that I don't— I don't care about being happy. I would rather know. There are a great many things—sad things assuredly—that I can't see, but you have no right to keep them from me. I have reflected a great deal during these winter months; I am afraid, you know, that the whole world is not as beautiful as you have made me believe, pastor—and, in fact, that it is very far from it."

"It is true that man has often defaced it," I argued timidly, for the rush of her thoughts frightened me and I tried to turn it aside, though without daring to hope I should succeed. She seemed to be waiting for these words, for she seized on them at once as though they were the missing link in the chain.

"Exactly!" she cried; "I want to be sure of not adding to the evil."

For a long time we walked on very quickly and in silence. Everything I might have said was checked beforehand by what I felt she was thinking; I dreaded to provoke some sentence that might set both our fates trembling in the balance. And as I thought of what Martins had said about the possibility of her regaining her sight, a dreadful anxiety gripped my heart.

"I wanted to ask you," she went on at last "—but I don't know how to say it. . . ."

Certainly she needed all her courage to speak, just as I needed all mine to listen. But how could I have foreseen the question that was tormenting her?

"Are the children of a blind woman necessarily born blind?"

I don't know which of us this conversation weighed down more, but it was necessary for us to go on.

"No, Gertrude," I said, "except in very special cases. There is in fact no reason why they should be."

She seemed extremely reassured. I should have liked in my turn to ask her why she wanted to know this; I had not the courage and went on clumsily:

"But, Gertrude, to have children, one must be married."

"Don't tell me that, pastor. I know it's not true."

"I have told you what it was proper for me to tell you," I protested. "But it is true, the laws of nature do allow what is forbidden by the laws of man and of God."

"You have often told me the laws of God were the laws of love."

"But such love as that is not the same that also goes by the name of charity."

"Is it out of charity you love me?"

"No, my Gertrude, you know it is not."

"Then you admit our love is outside the laws of God?"

"What do you mean?"

"Oh, you know well enough, and I ought not to be the one to say so."

I sought in vain for some way of evasion; the beating of my heart set all my arguments flying in confusion.

"Gertrude," I exclaimed wildly, "—you think your love wrong?"

She corrected me:

"*Our* love. . . . I say to myself I ought to think so."

"And then—?"

I heard what sounded like a note of supplication in my voice, while without waiting to take breath she went on:

"But that I cannot stop loving you."

All this happened yesterday. I hesitated at first to write it down. . . . I have no idea how our walk came to an end. We hurried along as if we were being pursued, while I held her arm tightly pressed against me. My soul was so absent from my body that I felt as if the smallest pebble in the path might send us both rolling to the ground.

19 May

Martins came back this morning. Gertrude's is a case for operation. Roux is certain of it and wishes to have her under his care for a time. I cannot refuse and yet, such is my cowardice, that I asked to be allowed to reflect. I asked to have time to prepare her gently. . . . My heart should leap for joy, but it feels inexpressibly heavy, weighed down by a sick misgiving. At the thought of having to tell Gertrude her sight may be restored to her, my heart fails me altogether.

19 May. Night

I have seen Gertrude and I have not told her. At the Grange this evening there was no one in the drawing-room; I went upstairs to her room. We were alone.

I held her long in my arms pressed to my heart. She made no attempt to resist, and as she raised her face to mine our lips met. . . .

21 May

O Lord, is it for us Thou hast clothed the night with such depth and such beauty? Is it for me? The air is warm and the moon shines in at my open window as I sit listening to the vast silence of the skies. Oh, from all creation rises a blended adoration that bears my heart along, lost in an ecstasy that knows no words. I cannot—I cannot pray with calm. If there is any limitation to love, it is set by man and not by Thee, my God. However guilty my love may appear in the eyes of men, oh, tell me that in Thine it is sacred.

I try to rise above the idea of sin; but sin seems to me intolerable, and I will not give up Christ. No, I will not admit that I sin in loving Gertrude. I could only succeed in tearing this love from my heart if I tore my heart out with it, and for what? If I did not already love her, it would be my duty to love her for pity's sake; to cease to love her would be to betray her; she needs my love. . . .

Lord, I know not. . . . I know nothing now but Thee. Be Thou my guide. Sometimes I feel that darkness is closing round me and that it is I who have been deprived of the sight that is to be restored to her.

Gertrude went into the Lausanne nursing-home yesterday and is not to come out for three weeks. I am expecting her return with extreme apprehension. Martins is to bring her back. She has made me promise not to try to see her before then.

22 May

A letter from Martins: the operation has been successful. God be thanked!

24 May

The idea that she who loved me without seeing me must now see me causes me intolerable discomfort. Will she know me? For the first time in my life I consult the mirror. If I feel her eyes are less indulgent than her heart and less loving, what will become of me? O Lord, I sometimes think I have need of her love in order to love Thee!

8 June

An unusual amount of work has enabled me to get through these last days with tolerable patience. Every occupation that takes me out of myself is a

merciful one; but all day long and through all that
happens her image is with me.

She is coming back tomorrow. Amélie, who during these last weeks has shown only the best side
of herself and seems endeavoring to distract my
thoughts, is preparing a little festivity with the children to welcome her return.

9 June

Gaspard and Charlotte have picked what flowers
they could find in the woods and fields. Old Rosalie
has manufactured a monumental cake, which Sarah
is decorating with gilt paper ornaments. We are
expecting her this morning for lunch.

I am writing to fill in the time of waiting. It is
eleven o'clock. Every moment I raise my head and
look out at the road along which Martins's carriage
will come. I resist the temptation to go and meet
them; it is better—especially for Amélie's sake—
that I should not welcome her apart from the others.
My heart leaps. . . . Ah, here they are!

9 June. Evening

Oh, in what abominable darkness I am plunged!
Pity, Lord, pity! I renounce loving her, but do
Thou not let her die!

How right my fears were! What has she done? What did she want to do? Amélie and Sarah tell me they went with her as far as the door of the Grange, where Mlle de la M. was expecting her. So she must have gone out again. . . . What happened?

I try to put my thoughts into some sort of order. The accounts they give are incomprehensible or contradictory. My mind is utterly confused . . . Mlle de la M.'s gardener has just brought her back to the Grange unconscious; he says he saw her walking by the river, then she crossed the garden bridge, then stooped and disappeared; but as he did not at first realize that she had fallen, he did not run to her help as he should have done; he found her at the little sluice, where she had been carried by the stream. When I saw her soon afterward, she had not recovered consciousness; or at least had lost it again, for she came to for a moment, thanks to the prompt measures that were taken. Martins, who, thank Heaven, had not yet left, cannot understand the kind of stupor and lassitude in which she is now sunk. He has questioned her in vain; she seems either not to hear or else to be determined not to speak. Her breathing is very labored and Martins is afraid of pneumonia; he has ordered sinapisms and cupping and has promised to come

again tomorrow. The mistake was leaving her too
long in her wet clothes while they were trying to
bring her round; the water of the river is icy. Mlle
de la M., who is the only person who has succeeded
in getting a few words from her, declares she wanted
to pick some of the forget-me-nots that grow in
abundance on this side of the river, and that,
being still unaccustomed to measure distances, or
else mistaking the floating carpet of flowers for
solid ground, she suddenly lost her footing. . . .
If I could only believe it! If I could only persuade
myself it was nothing but an accident, what a dreadful load would be lifted from my heart! During the
whole meal, though it was so gay, the strange smile
that never left her face made me uneasy; a forced
smile, which I had never seen her wear before, but
which I tried my utmost to believe was the smile
of her newly born sight; a smile that seemed to
stream from her eyes onto her face like tears, and
beside which the vulgar mirth of the others seemed
to me offensive. She did not join in the mirth; I felt
as if she had discovered a secret she would surely
have confided to me if we had been alone. She
hardly spoke; but no one was surprised at that,
because she is often silent when she is with others,
and all the more so when their merriment grows
noisy.

Lord, I beseech Thee, let me speak to her. I must know or how can I continue to live? . . . And yet if she really wished to end her life, is it just because she *knew*? Knew what? Dear, what horrible thing can you have learned? What did I hide from you that was so deadly? What can you so suddenly have seen?

I have been spending two hours at her bedside, my eyes never leaving her forehead, her pale cheeks, her delicate eyelids, shut down over some unspeakable sorrow, her hair still wet and like seaweed as it lies spread round her on the pillow—listening to her difficult, irregular breathing.

10 June

Mlle Louise sent for me this morning just as I was starting to go to the Grange. After a fairly quiet night Gertrude has at last emerged from her torpor. She smiled when I went into the room and motioned to me to come and sit by her bedside. I did not dare question her, and no doubt she was dreading my questions, for she said immediately, as though to forestall anything emotional:

"What do you call those little blue flowers that I wanted to pick by the river? Flowers the color of the sky. Will you be cleverer than I and pick me a bunch of them? I should like to have them here beside my bed. . . ."

The false cheerfulness of her voice was dreadful to me; and no doubt she was aware of it, for she added more gravely:

"I can't speak to you this morning; I am too tired. Go and pick those flowers for me, will you? You can come back again later."

And when an hour later I brought her the bunch of forget-me-nots, Mlle Louise told me that Gertrude was resting and could not see me before evening.

I saw her again this evening. She was lying— almost sitting up in bed—propped against a pile of pillows. Her hair was now fastened up, with the forget-me-nots I had brought her twisted into the plaits above her forehead.

She was obviously very feverish and drew her breath with great difficulty. She kept the hand I put out to her in her burning hand; I remained standing beside her.

"I must confess something to you, pastor; because this evening I am afraid of dying," she said. "What I told you this morning was a lie. It was not to pick flowers. . . . Will you forgive me if I say I wanted to kill myself?"

I fell on my knees beside the bed, still keeping

her frail hand in mine; but she disengaged it and began to stroke my forehead, while I buried my face in the sheets so as to hide my tears and stifle my sobs.

"Do you think it was very wrong?" she went on tenderly; then, as I answered nothing:

"My friend, my friend," she said, "you must see that I take up too much room in your heart and in your life. When I came back to you, that was what struck me at once—or, at any rate, that the place I took belonged to another and that it made her unhappy. My crime is that I did not feel it sooner; or rather—for indeed I knew it all along—that I allowed you to love me in spite of it. But when her face suddenly appeared to me, when I saw such unhappiness on her poor face, I could not bear the idea that that unhappiness was my work. . . . No, no, don't blame yourself for anything; but let me go, and give her back her joy."

The hand ceased stroking my forehead; I seized it and covered it with kisses and tears. But she drew it away impatiently and began to toss in the throes of some fresh emotion.

"That is not what I wanted to say to you; no, it's not that I want to say," she kept repeating, and I saw the sweat on her damp forehead. Then she closed her eyes and kept them shut for a time, as though to concentrate her thoughts or to recover her former state of blindness; and in a voice that at first was trailing and mournful, but that soon, as she reopened her eyes, grew louder, grew at last animated even to vehemence:

"When you gave me back my sight," she began, "my eyes opened on a world more beautiful than I had ever dreamed it could be; yes, truly, I had never imagined the daylight so bright, the air so brilliant, the sky so vast. But I had never imagined men's faces so full of care either; and when I went into your house, do you know what it was that struck me first? . . . Oh, it can't be helped, I must tell you: what I saw first of all was our fault, our sin. No, don't protest. You remember Christ's words: 'If ye were blind ye should have no sin.' But now I see. . . . Get up, pastor. Sit there, beside me. Listen to me without interrupting. During the time I spent in the nursing-home I read—or rather I had read to me some verses of the Bible I did not know —some you had never read me. I remember a text of St. Paul's which I repeated to myself all one day: 'For I was alive without the law once; but when the commandment came, sin revived, and I died.' "

She spoke in a state of extreme excitement and in a very loud voice, almost shouting the last words, so that I was made uncomfortable by the idea that they might be heard outside the room; then she shut her eyes and repeated in a whisper, as though for herself alone:

"Sin revived—and *I* died."

I shivered and my heart froze in a kind of terror. I tried to turn aside her thoughts.

"Who read you those texts?" I asked.

"Jacques," she said, opening her eyes and looking at me fixedly. "Did you know he was converted?"

It was more than I could bear; I was going to implore her to stop, but she had already gone on:

"My friend, I am going to grieve you very much; but there must be no falsehood between us now. When I saw Jacques, I suddenly realized it was not you I loved—but him. He had your face—I mean the face I imagined you had. . . . Ah! why did you make me refuse him? I might have married him. . . ."

"But, Gertrude, you still can," I cried with despair in my heart.

"He is entering the priesthood," she said impetuously. Then, shaken by sobs: "Oh, I want to confess to him," she moaned in a kind of ecstasy. . . . "You see for yourself there's nothing left me but to die. I am thirsty. Please call someone. I can't breathe. Leave me. I want to be alone. Ah! I had hoped that speaking to you would have brought me more relief. You must say good-by. We must say good-by. I cannot bear to be with you any more."

I left her. I called Mlle de la M. to take my place beside her; her extreme agitation made me fear the worst, but I could not help seeing that my presence did her harm. I begged that I might be sent for if there was a change for the worse.

11 June

Alas! I was never to see her again alive. She died this morning after a night of delirium and exhaustion. Jacques, who at Gertrude's dying request was telegraphed for by Mlle de la M., arrived a few hours after the end. He reproached me cruelly for not having called in a priest while there was yet time. But how could I have done so when I was still unaware that during her stay at Lausanne, and evidently urged by him, Gertrude had abjured the Protestant faith? He told me in the same breath of his own conversion and Gertrude's. And so they both left me at the same time; it seemed as if, separated by me during their lifetime, they had planned to escape me here and be united to each other in

God. But I tell myself that Jacques's conversion is more a matter of the head than the heart.

"Father," he said, "it is not fitting for me to make accusations against you; but it was the example of your error that guided me."

After Jacques had left again, I knelt down beside Amélie and asked her to pray for me, as I was in need of help. She simply repeated "Our Father . . ." but after each sentence she left long pauses, which we filled with our supplication.

I would have wept, but I felt my heart more arid than the desert.

A NOTE ABOUT THE AUTHOR

ANDRÉ GIDE was born in Paris in 1869, and received a strict Protestant education in that city. His first literary works, in his early twenties, established him as a promising member of the new symbolist group; but in 1895, after a voyage of self-discovery in North Africa, he turned to the glorification of life and liberty in works close to the spirit of Nietzsche and Walt Whitman. With Paris and his Norman estate as headquarters, Gide spent much of his life restlessly traveling throughout Europe and Africa while devoting himself entirely to literary creation.

By the time *The Counterfeiters* appeared (1926) Gide's reputation was solidly established on such brief fictions as *Strait Is the Gate* and *The Immoralist,* on several highly original plays, and on the most penetrating literary criticism of the epoch.

After World War II new works by Gide, including his celebrated *Journals,* continued to appear, and he remained an incredibly young spirit, a leader among those dominating contemporary European letters. He was awarded the Nobel Prize for Literature in 1947. In 1950 he was made an Honorary Corresponding Member of the American Academy of Arts and Letters. André Gide died in Paris on February 19, 1951.

VINTAGE BELLES—LETTRES

VINTAGE POLITICAL SCIENCE AND SOCIAL CRITICISM

V-862 **HUNNIUS, GERRY, DAVID G. GARSON AND JOHN CASE** / Workers Control: A Reader on Labor and Social Change

V-514 **HUNTINGTON, SAMUEL F.** / The Soldier and the State

V-566 **HURLEY, ROGER** / Poverty & Mental Retardation: A Causal Relationship

V-17 **JAFFE, DENNIS AND TED CLARKE (eds.)** / Worlds Apart: Young People and The Drug Programs

V-241 **JACOBS, JANE** / Death and Life of Great American Cities

V-584 **JACOBS, JANE** / The Economy of Cities

V-433 **JACOBS, PAUL** / Prelude to Riot

V-459 **JACOBS, PAUL AND SAUL LANDAU WITH EVE PELL** / To Serve the Devil: Natives and Slaves Vol. I

V-460 **JACOBS, PAUL AND SAUL LANDAU WITH EVE PELL** / To Serve the Devil: Colonials and Sojourners Vol. II

V-2017 **JUDSON, HORACE FREELAND** / Heroin Addiction: What Americans Can Learn from the English Experience

V-790 **KAPLAN, CAROL AND LAWRENCE (eds.)** / Revolutions, A Comparative Study

V-337 **KAUFMANN, WALTER (trans.) AND FRIEDRICH NIETZSCHE** / Beyond Good and Evil

V-369 **KAUFMANN, WALTER (trans.) AND FRIEDRICH NIETZSCHE** / The Birth of Tragedy and The Case of Wagner

V-985 **KAUFMANN, WALTER (trans.) AND FRIEDRICH NIETZSCHE** / The Gay Science

V-401 **KAUFMANN, WALTER (trans.) AND FRIEDRICH NIETZSCHE** / On the Genealogy of Morals and Ecce Homo

V-437 **KAUFMANN, WALTER (trans.) AND FRIEDRICH NIETZSCHE** / The Will to Power

V-994 **KELLNER, HANSFRIED AND PETER AND BRIGITTE BERGER** / The Homeless Mind: Modernization and Consciousness

V-482 **KELSO, LOUIS O. AND PATRICIA HETTER** / Two-Factor Theory: The Economics of Reality

V-708 **KESSLE, GUN AND JAN MYRDAL** / China: The Revolution Continued

V-510 **KEY, V. O.** / Southern Politics

V-764 **KLARE, MICHAEL T.** / War Without End: American Planning for the Next Vietnams

V-981 **KLINE, MORRIS** / Why Johnny Can't Add: The Failure of the New Math

V-361 **KOMAROVSKY, MIRRA** / Blue Collar Marriage

V-675 **KOVEL, JOVEL** / White Racism

V-459 **LANDAU, SAUL, PAUL JACOBS WITH EVE PELL** / To Serve the Devil: Natives and Slaves Vol. I

V-460 **LANDAU, SAUL, PAUL JACOBS WITH EVE PELL** / To Serve the Devil: Colonials and Sojourners Vol. II

V-560 **LASCH, CHRISTOPHER** / The Agony of the American Left

V-367 **LASCH, CHRISTOPHER** / The New Radicalism in America

V-46 **LASCH, CHRISTOPHER** / The World of Nations

V-987 **LEKACHMANN, ROBERT** / Inflation: The Permanent Problem of Boom and Bust

V-880 **LERNER, GERDA (ed.)** / Black Women in White America: A Documentary History

V-280 **LEWIS, OSCAR** / The Children of Sanchez